Table of Contents

Front & Back Covers by Laura Givens

Diversity in Speculative Fiction

There's a debate underway about diversity in speculative fiction. Are women sufficiently well represented? Do we hear enough African-American voices? Do trans-gendered people have a say? To my mind, presenting a diverse range of viewpoints, voices, and styles is the whole reason for collecting stories from multiple authors into a magazine or anthology.

In the twenty years *Tales of the Talisman* and *Hadrosaur Tales* have been published, one of our driving principals is that everyone who submits has an equal chance of being selected. In fact, we typically set cover letters aside and do our best to read and evaluate stories without paying attention to who submitted them. We endeavor to select stories and poetry based on their quality alone.

Admittedly, the editorial team are white Americans, with all the biases thereof, but we attempt to pick stories that challenge our worldviews as well as those which support them. Another thing that makes this system imperfect is that we have to do business with the contributors. We need names and contact information so we can accept or reject stories. As a result, the submission process is never truly blind. We're also limited by who chooses to submit.

This issue contains stories, poems, and artwork from four continents. I've corresponded with many of the authors and I know we do have a diverse range of voices. That said, looking at the contents of this issue, it's clear there are more men than women represented. That alone demonstrates our process is imperfect.

This is the next to last issue before *Tales of the Talisman* goes on hiatus. I actually prefer to say that we're going into a chrysalis phase. When we come out, Hadrosaur Productions will still publish short fiction and poetry, but in way that's more sustainable for me with my other careers as writer and astronomer. I would also like to find ways to present an even more diverse range of voices. This might include working with other editors and encouraging those who wouldn't normally submit to a speculative fiction market to give it a try. If you have any ideas, please drop me a note at hadrosaur@zianet.com

In the meantime, turn the page and see what this collection of authors has to say.

— David Lee Summers
Las Cruces, NM

Tales of the
Talisman

Volume 10   Issue 3

ISBN: 1-885093-78-0

William Grother
Publisher

David Lee Summers
Editor

Laura Givens
Art Director

Kumie Wise
Assistant Editor

Tales of the Talisman
(ISSN 1558-0377)
is published quarterly by
Hadrosaur Productions
P.O. Box 2194
Mesilla Park, NM 88047-2194
www.hadrosaur.com

Subscriptions: $24.00 per year
$48.00 per two years
Subscriptions available at:
www.talesofthetalisman.com

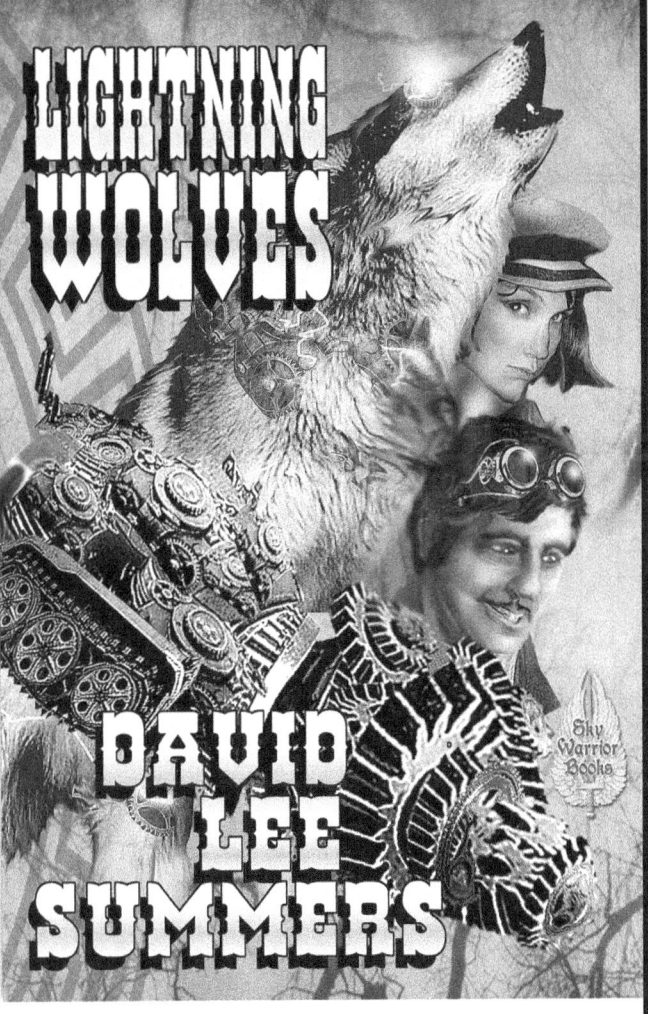

Cerulean Dream

Story by Lou Antonelli
Illustration by Kathy Ferrell

It was a week after the 17th St. Canal levee had breached—and a month since my mother died—and I was still in the house.

Lakeview had flooded; there were no other people left on the block. I was living on the second floor. Of course the electricity was off but strangely enough the gas was still flowing and the cook stove in the kitchen still worked.

As bizarre as it was, that morning I went downstairs—where there was three feet of standing water—and made breakfast. I had found an old metal percolator in the attic, and I used cast iron skillets. There was bread in the pantry, and bacon and eggs that I kept cold inside the waterlogged refrigerator.

I know it sounds strange that I would stand there in three feet of stagnant water, cooking—but the whole scene of devastation caused by Hurricane Katrina was surreal.

That morning as I cooked for myself I heard a gentle splashing in the street and looked out to see a young lady in a flowing dress had stopped in front of the house. I could see she was sniffing, and I thought, "She must be hungry."

She also looked very much lost. I went to the door, and called out "Do need some food?" She looked at me strangely and didn't say anything, but came closer.

"Do you need something to eat?"

As she came up to the gate I could see her dress was clinging to her body as if she'd been completely immersed. Her skin was pale like she hadn't seen much sunlight. Her hair was extraordinarily black, and her eyes a most bright and unusual shade of blue. I couldn't recall ever having seen that shade before.

I motioned for her to come in. "You don't need to be wandering the streets alone, young lady," I said. "Come here, I have some food."

She still didn't speak but came to the house. She looked around as she stood inside the door, amazed at the sight. There was water three feet high throughout the first floor, with all the furniture still sitting there. I thought to myself it looked nothing so much as like a boat that was half sunk.

I went back to the stove where I had some toast on an iron skillet. I had to take the percolator off the stove before it boiled over. When I turned my attention back to her, I realized she was very, very beautiful.

Under normal circumstances I would think it improper for an old bachelor like me just to invite the young lady inside, but these weren't normal circumstances. She sniffed and looked at the stove like she

was very hungry. She also seemed to watch the gas flame like it was a living creature.

I turned back to the stove. "I still have a few eggs," I said. "I've been saving them. Would you like some scrambled eggs?"

She looked at me inquisitively but still didn't speak and it occurred to me she might not speak English.

"Parlez vous Francais? Habla Espanol?" I asked. "Kenst reden Yiddish?"

Still nothing. "Or she just might be a mute," I thought.

I forgot about the eggs; the bacon had finished cooking. I put some butter on toast and two slices of bacon on the butter. I handed it to her. She did look a little thin.

"Here you go young lady," I said.

She gingerly picked the bacon up and ate each slice, and then licked the butter off the bread before breaking the toast into pieces and eating it.

"Definitely a foreigner," I thought.

I drank my coffee and looked at her. "Do you have some place to stay?"

No reaction. Well, I knew the National Guard had a high-wheeled vehicle that drove down the street every so often to check on the few people, such as myself, who were still in their homes in the neighborhood. The next time it came down the street, I would flag it down and make sure they took her along.

She seemed attentive enough, although somewhat shy, and I hadn't had anyone to talk to in over a week. "I live in Shreveport," I said. "I've lived there 30 years. I grew up in this house, and my mother still lived here, until she died last month. My father died a long time ago. After mom's funeral, I came here to organize things and prepare for selling the house."

I looked at her. "And then Katrina came to visit."

She seemed to be listening. "I didn't want to leave the house, not that there is anything terribly valuable, but there are a lot of things here that are very personal. The second story is still warm and dry. I've been up there since the 17th St. Canal wall opened up."

"I have a battery-powered radio, and I've been staying in a bedroom upstairs," I continued. "Things are in chaos in the city. If you have no place to go, you can stay here until the next National Guard patrol comes by."

As I said that I looked at the staircase and her

gaze followed mine.

"Why the hell are we standing here in the water? I'm going back upstairs. You can come and dry out."

I finished my coffee and toast and climbed up the stairs. At this point I really didn't know if the strange pretty girl would accept my invitation, but I didn't care.

I was almost to the top when I heard the creaking that indicated she was following me. "Watch your step," I said. "It's slippery." I looked back and down and saw her legs and feet were pink like a newborn baby's.

Although the first floor looked like a derelict ship, the second-floor looked as normal as ever. I went into the guest bedroom—which many years before had been my bedroom—and pulled a rocking chair by the front window so I could keep a watch out for the National Guard.

She came into the room and looked all around in wonder. "She's either a foreigner or really poor," I thought. "Or both. This isn't that special a place."

I gestured for her sit down on the bed. She did, then she lay down, and fell fast asleep.

"Poor thing," I thought. "God knows what she's been through. Perhaps her family is dead." I took a quilt off the rack and covered her with it.

* * *

The National Guard truck came down the street but I didn't have the heart to wake the young lady. I felt a certain sense of protectiveness, and I sat by the window the rest of the day.

I didn't realize I had fallen asleep, but then I felt a gentle tugging at my sleeve. The girl was there, trying to get my attention like a friendly dog. I looked over to an old mechanical alarm clock on the dresser, and could see it was 6 p.m.

She was kneeling on the floor. I leaned on the arm of the rocking chair. "Listen young lady," I said. "I'm happy to give you shelter, but it's about time you explained yourself a little bit. Hurricane or no hurricane, things might seem improper—especially since I'm single and you are so young."

I pointed a finger at my chest. "My name is Larry," I said. "What is your name?" I asked, pointing the finger at her.

Her eyes widened. She finally spoke. "Azura," she said.

"Okay," I said. "Now, we're getting someplace."

I made an expansive circle in the air with my finger and hand. "This is New Orleans," I said. Then I pointed at her. "Are you from New Orleans?"

She shook her head.

I made a very wide circle in the air. "So where are you from?" I asked.

She looked at me as if thinking real hard, and said something that sounded like "Azitilan".

There was a large reproduction of an old lithograph map of The Confederacy on the wall as a decoration. I went over to it and rubbed my hand flat across.

"Are you from any place around here?" I asked.

She stood up and came over to me. She looked at me, and looked at the map.

She pointed—right at the center of the Gulf of Mexico.

I was so startled my knees buckled. I looked at her, and realized what I had refused to recognize before.

She looked at me and for the first time she smiled. She knew that I knew.

I couldn't believe it. She kneeled beside me and then held herself up against me. She started to nibble on my neck and we both fell down on the floor.

In a moment, we were making love, and soon everything turned white and I fainted dead away.

* * *

I woke up as the sun streamed through the window the next morning. I was sore, and as I got on my knees and then rose unsteadily, I thought to myself, "That couldn't have been real."

She was nowhere to be found. "Wow, that was the strangest dream."

I dressed, and went down to the kitchen, and I found the two plates still on the counter.

I looked out the kitchen window over the vast expanse of water, and thought "This water goes unbroken out towards the Gulf. I wonder whether, in this calamity that struck us, there are also victims we don't know about—victims who were driven inland from beneath the sea."

I heard a splashing and rumbling from the street, and saw the National Guard truck stop in front of my house. A guardsman shouted.

"You have to evacuate now," he hollered. "It's mandatory."

I went to the door. "What about looters?"

"Guardsmen are coming in from all states, he said. "Patrols have increased. Everything will be safe."

"Give me a few minutes, and I'll get my clothes," I said.

As I ran upstairs, I looked into the master bedroom, where I had organized some of my parents' stuff. I realized I probably stayed because of the sense of loss and the need for closure. I was an only child.

I supposed it was time to move on.

"This stuff can wait," I said to no one. I threw what I needed into a knapsack, closed all the windows and locked the front door on my way out.

I waded out to the truck, and hopped in the back. As we drove away, I looked across the water and wondered about Azura.

* * *

It's been almost ten years now, and I pretty much came to think of the whole episode as some kind of bizarre dream.

The renovation of the family home took so much time and expense that I left my apartment in Shreveport and moved back in permanently. I was fortunate to find a good job in New Orleans, which greatly facilitated the move.

As part of the renovation I completely overhauled the first floor. Obviously the kitchen had to be gutted and refurbished. It's very nice now. So this morning I'm cooking breakfast alone as usual—in a nice dry kitchen, not standing in three feet of water—when I see someone who looks vaguely familiar walking down the sidewalk.

I lean towards the window and see it is just a little girl—but something had momentarily fooled my eye. Her hair was lustrous and black, and she carried a gym bag. She looked at the house, stopped at the gate and opened it.

I went to the door and opened it. She just stood there and made no effort to ring the doorbell.

"Hello young lady," I said through the glass. "Can I help you?"

Her eyes were a familiar shade of cerulean blue, with flecks of greenish-gray that reminded me of sea foam.

"Are you Larry?" she asked.

"Yes, I am," I said. "Who are you?"

"I am Schiara," she said. "Daughter of Azura. I have come to live with you."

I open the door quickly and stared hard at her. She was very young but looked me in the eye. "My mother said I must come to stay with you, for I am more of your people that I am of hers," she said.

I was stunned. "I am an old bachelor," I said. "I have no family and I have no children."

"Yes, you do," she said. She gave me a look and I got out of the way. She stepped inside and she dropped the gym bag on the floor.

I looked at her hard and recognized a lot.

"Your mother was much shyer and a lot less talkative than you," I said in amazement.

"That's because she said I *am* like you," she said. She sniffed and looked towards the kitchen.

"What's for breakfast?"

I raised my arms in a gesture of resignation. "Bacon and eggs and toast, with coffee." I said.

"Great," she said as she sat at the table. "It's been a long trip, and I'm hungry."

I went over to the coffeemaker, looked back at her, and I just couldn't keep from laughing at her audacity.

She smiled and laughed too.

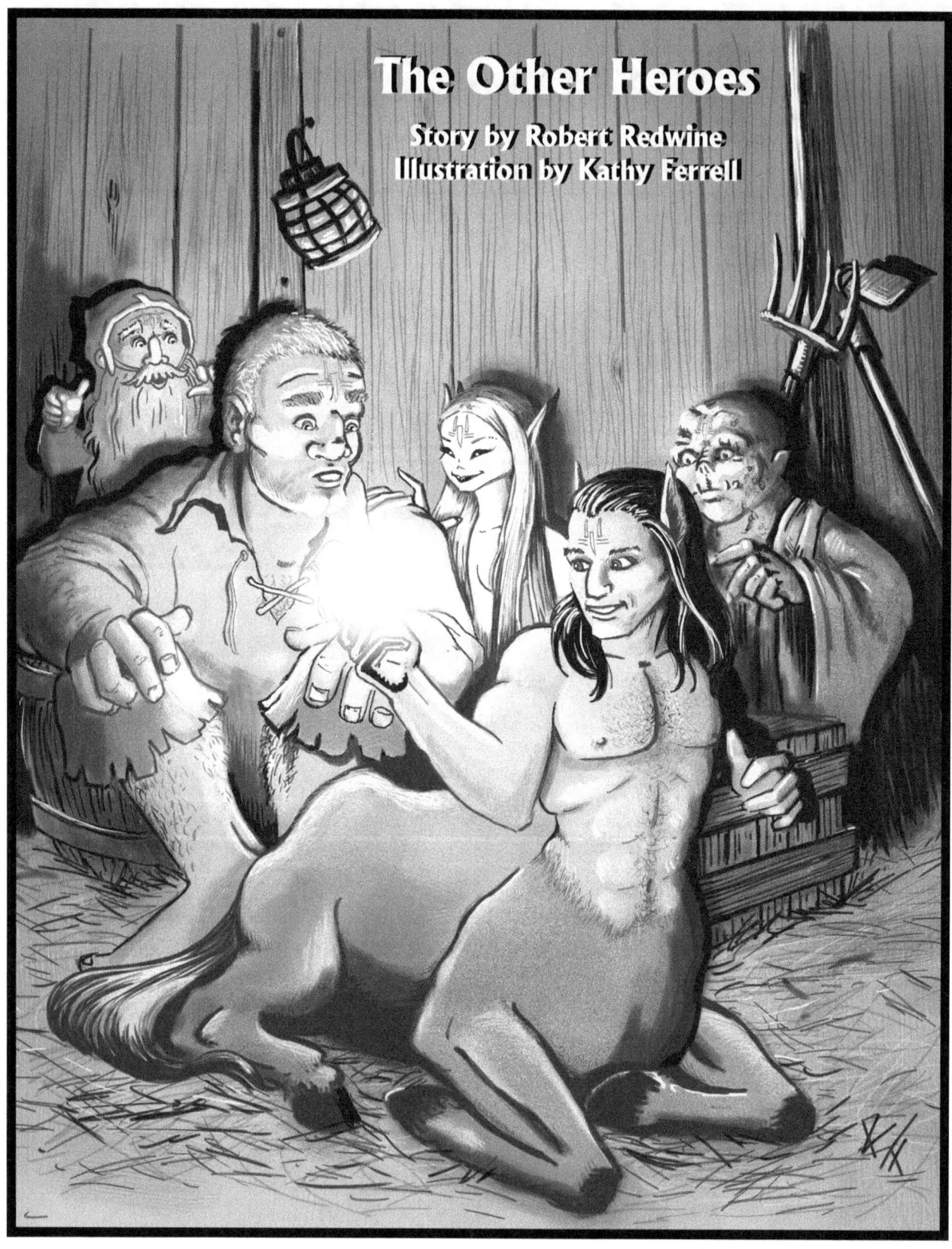

The Other Heroes

Story by Robert Redwine
Illustration by Kathy Ferrell

Storyteller? Are there *any groups of heroes that do not include humans?*

Silence fell around the fire. Youngsters shifted uncomfortably as the old Storyteller put down his drink. "It is true," said the Storyteller, "That many of my stories center around humans. Of all the races, they seem to be the most driven. And that gets them into trouble that makes good stories. But the Gods do choose others to be heroes…"

* * *

"Waitress! Another round!" roared Mohg. He slammed the bucket that served as his mug onto the table. The other patrons in the common room sidled away from the giant and his friends.

"Come on. Eat up! We earned it," he continued as he grabbed a roasted turkey leg. His fourth so far.

"If I eat any more, I will burst," said Willow. A bare arm slid out of the slit of her cloak to brush honey-blond hair over an elfin ear. Mohg was surprised she had not already grabbed a male or two to take back to her room. Under that cloak, she wore not a stitch.

Another bucket-mug hit the table, this one now emptied of water. G'herron, a centaur nearly as massive as Mohg, reached for a loaf of fresh bread. Unlike others the giant had met, this centaur drank only water and ate no meat. He also had the annoying habit of saying little except for mystical proverbs.

"Careful where you wave that, please," said Hur from the seat next to Mohg. He waved a few chunks of turkey and grease off his gleaming white robes. Mohg thought they clashed with his orcish features. Still, the orc was the kindest being the giant knew. The heart of the party.

The barwench shrieked as she finished setting down the round of drinks. Wil, the last member of the band, chuckled gruffly and reached for a tankard of ale. A typical dwarf male, or so the act went. Bruwilde was no more male than Willow, and a wizard to boot. Mohg wished she were about six feet taller.

He dropped a scattering of coins on the wench's tray. Her smile suggested that if he were only half his size… And for a bit more it may not be a barrier. Maybe he would consider that. If his money-bag were heavier.

But he was the only one with any real attention to coin. G'herron, raised by warrior-monks, cared little for money. Willow had no pockets. Hur would give most of it to the poor, leaving them poor themselves' And Wil would find some expensive book and forget to eat. They all bore the Mark of the Gods; he figured he was there to keep them all alive. And to do that, he would need more coin.

After supper, they separated. G'herron to the stables, the others to their rooms, and Mohg off into the night. Time to pick a few pockets; after all, he was a thief.

Westtower was a trade city, and trade meant coin in plenty. The Gods had not yet led them into more mortal peril, and such adventures were always expensive. Still, it was easier than being a farmer. He hated work.

As he stalked the dark alleys, he stepped past the poor and desperate. No concern of his. Hur had the bleeding heart, not him. At each intersection, he stopped and listened.

An hour later he heard the wonderful sound of coins changing hands. It began with a thump, followed by dragging sounds. Over the cycles, he had learned that city thieves tended to carry the most ready coin. And be the poorest fighters. He hated the sight of blood, especially his own. He moved closer.

Two humans dragged a fourth. The third watched the larger street in the opposite direction. Mohg waited until they were done searching their victim and backing away. Right toward him. In the dark, he looked like a bulge in the building wall.

It was his kind of fight. Grossly unfair in his favor. No 'honorable' call to surrender. No announcing of intent. Just sneaky thumps on two of them, and when the third turned at the sound, Mohg wedgied him into unconsciousness. Unintentionally. His trousers were better made than expected.

Mohg picked pockets by ripping off anything with a pocket. Much more efficient than searching while in dark alleys. The now-rags went into a large pouch. Two blocks later he ran into trouble.

The rooftops seemed to sprout humans with crossbows. Another slid out of the shadows in front of him, holding a sword. He was outnumbered at least ten to one, and they had the drop on him. But there was hope; they had not simply opened fire. Maybe he could talk his way out of this.

"Well. Well. Well," said the human. "You are a long way from your friends. And you have not paid your dues to the Guild. How disappointing."

"Dues?" said the giant. "Of course! I knew I forgot something. So, what are the Guild Rates? I just came into some coin."

"We do not steal from brothers. I am afraid the dues for you will be both your thumbs." He started forward. "Refuse, and it will be your head."

Something moved nearby, glowing white in the light of the three moons. A blade so large even he would have trouble with mowed through the archers on his left. From his right, it started raining thieves. Mohg kicked the swordsman into a wall. Seconds later, the fight was over.

"Reach too often into the honeycomb, and the bees get annoyed," came the sing-song voice of G'herron. From a rooftop. How had the centaur, over a ton of centaur, gotten up there? And not crashed through the roof?

"Can we do it again?" said Willow from the other roof. "It really was not fair, even with me running in front of them before attacking." Her sword, magically clean, lay on her bare shoulder. It was larger than she in both length and width, and probably weighed more than she did. She only wore a smile. Disgusting. If only she had more hair like Wil, and another thousand pounds or so.

Mohg collected more pockets. He avoided Willow's 'opponents' as much as he could. By the time he was done, the elf and centaur joined him. She had vanished her sword and put on her cloak. G'herron's hooves clopped on the cobblestones.

"All right, what brought you two out here?" he said.

"He did," said Willow. "Though when he said exercise, I had hoped for something else." She winked. "He will give in eventually. But this was not too bad. Gets the blood pumping." Her voice lowered to a purr. "Want to help me cool down?"

"No thank you," said Mohg. "I guess this means it is time to return to the inn?"

The centaur tossed one of the crossbows to Mohg. He examined it curiously. Then he saw the black tar on the bolt. Poison, and a lot of it. These men were not playing around. Definitely time to go back to the inn. Besides, he needed to sort his loot.

Willow passed inside while the giant and centaur went into the stables. None of the interior rooms had sufficient space for the pair. They shared a massive stall meant for a full wagon-team. Mohg threw a blanket over a double-thick stack of hay bales. G'herron settled onto the fresh hay on the floor and closed his eyes.

The giant sat and started emptying his pouches onto his impromptu table. At least the haul was good. Plenty of silver coins with the occasional gold made heaps on the blanket. He also found vials, a few small jars, assorted jewelry, and parchments.

The parchments troubled Mohg. Most were pictures of him and his friends. Others had orders to observe, separate, and capture them. And a large

reward in gold when it was done. So that was why they did not kill him outright.

In a thick black velvet bag that came from the swordsman's pouches, he found a crystal sphere. He had no magical aptitude, but it made the hair on his hand stand up when he touched it. He would show it to Wil in the morning. Maybe it was worth a lot of money.

He put the valuables away. The personal items, bits of wire and tools, and useless junk went into a waste bucket. He rolled up in his blanket on the bed of hay bales.

He had nothing to worry about as he fell into sleep. G'herron, even while meditating, was more aware than Mohg at his best. And centaurs did not sleep.

* * *

Bruwilde affixed her fake beard. She only took it off when well-protected. A word and gesture unlocked and opened her spellbook. She took a deep breath and began preparing her mind for magic.

An hour later she was ready to join the others for breakfast. Behind her eyes, the magic sang in her mind. A Stroke of Lightning begged for release. A Shield promised protection. Other spells added their voices to the harmony. She wondered when she would find another spell to add to the chorus.

Bruwilde let the Sound Barrier drop. She had learned months ago to use one when she shared a wall with Willow. She was just as enthusiastic with her bed partners as she was on the battlefield. Thankfully, no noise came through the now-unprotected wall. She left her room behind for steak and eggs.

"Hey Wil," said Mohg. She looked up. The giant was lazy, a glutton, and almost as much a hedonist as Willow. But not bad, as giants went. "Can you take a look at this?"

She caught the black velvet sack and peeked inside. She had to blink and look away for a moment. There was powerful magic within. She was used to the magic around her friends, but new magic was another story. She pulled out the crystal sphere.

It glowed with an inner light that reflected off the Marks of her companions. She still remembered the day the god Worfess had stuck the Mark on her own forehead with his enchanted Minting Press. A Mark that bound them to a common fate. She looked deeper into the sphere.

"Where did you get this?" she growled.

"Found it, along with some potions, on some guys that tried to rob me," said Mohg. Willow giggled and G'herron sighed. Bruwilde knew there was more to the story. With him, there always was. And the more she pressed, the less truth she would get.

"Did these 'guys' have anything else on them? Just cough it up. And give me the potions so I can identify them."

"Yes Wil," said the giant after a moment. He passed a satchel-sized pouch over. She was surprised at how easily he gave in. Maybe he was finally seeing reason.

Inside the pouch were a group of portraits and instructions on their capture. Along with potion vials in padded pockets. She sorted through them quickly and passed around the parchments.

"They missed my birthmark," said Willow. "And made my breasts too large."

"But they have a good likeness of your sword," said Hur. "And the rest of them are good as well. We should find the artist and have portraits done."

"Only you would find a good point to finding out a new group of people want to kill us," said Mohg.

"But these say capture," said Willow.

"So they can kill us later," said Mohg.

"Or perhaps give us to the demon," said Bruwilde.

Silence fell. The pleasant smile slid off Hur's face. G'herron set down his drink. Willow started to look excited.

"Demon?" said Mohg.

"Yes," she said. "And a powerful one."

"An untended flower grows too large to manage," said the centaur. Mohg put his face in his hands.

"He's right," said Bruwilde. "We should deal with this quickly. It may already know we know."

"Yaay! Action!" said Willow. "When do we leave?"

"It is not that simple," said the dwarf. "We need to figure out where it is. Until then, I suggest none of us goes out alone."

"The resources of the White Temple are at your disposal," said Hur. "I shall accompany you."

"G'herron, can you keep Mohg and Willow out of trouble while we are gone?"

"When faced with the unscalable mountain, one must still make the attempt."

The elf nudged the giant and winked. Bruwilde did not envy the centaur. She shouldered the satchel and stood. Hur, topping her by well over a foot, joined her.

As they walked to the temple, Hur drew eyes. One did not normally find an orc in a 'civilized' setting. Even less in the company of a dwarf warrior, Wil's disguise. She knew one end of her hammer from the other, but even Mohg was a better fighter.

"I cannot believe such a beast walks free," said a passer-by.

"What manner of dwarf would associate with *that*?"

"It must have killed an Orudarran priest for his robes."

A few went so far as to jostle the priest, who only replied with, "Light shield you." She breathed a sigh of relief when they reached the White Temple.

The Temple of Orudarr glowed where white marble and glass met sunshine. He was one of the three gods of magic, representing magic used to benefit all. The doorwards looked dubiously at Hur. Their eyes widened when they saw his silver book pendant.

"Please brothers, let us pass," said the orc. She again marveled at his restraint. She was tempted to correct their attitudes with her hammer, if only to salve his dignity. He deserved better. The doorwards stood firm.

"I think you have to prove it to them," said Wil.

"I can understand their doubt." He muttered a short prayer and erupted in an aura of light. She knew it was harmless to them, and no novice magic.

"Apologies, Librarian," said the doorward on the left with a bow. The other bowed as well.

"Accepted. You were only doing your duty," said Hur as the aura faded away. He started forward. Bruwilde followed. The marble doors opened at their approach. An acolyte met them.

"We need the demon section of the library," said the dwarf. The acolyte looked at her like the doorwards had watched Hur. He opened his mouth to give the lists of rules.

"I already know the rules," she snapped. "I never get treated like this at the Grey Tower."

Hur laid his hand on her shoulder. If only she had his patience. The acolyte bowed hastily and led them inside. She decided not to add the acolyte to her Book of Grudges. They arrived at the appropriate section a short time later.

"How about I identify the potions while you research the demon?" said Hur.

"That works," she said. She pulled out the sphere and looked at it again. This time she called up one of her spells. With a word, she finished the internal song and released the power.

Her vision altered. The waves of Power imbuing the sphere swirled around it. Definitely a communication sphere, not just a conduit of demonic power. If the demon were slain, it would become very useful. For now, it served to help track and identify the demon. She called for scrolls and tomes.

Hours, and three acolytes later, she closed her journal and gave the scrolls back to the attendant. Hur was nowhere to be seen. She stopped the departing acolyte.

"Where would Librarian Hur test the potions?"

"Librarian Hur left a short time ago."

"What?" Her hand fell to her component pouch. She rarely relied on the hammer on her belt. She hustled to the entrance of the Temple. There was no sign of him. Her swearing nearly made the doorwards faint.

She used another spell. Time seemed to reverse. All the people on the street walked and talked backwards. She hoped a 'short time' was within her Looking Back spell. She squinted as past and present collided in her field of view. She saw Hur walking backwards toward her with a pair of humans.

She let the Looking Back spell start catching up with the now and set off after them. She bumped and shoved through the crowd, leaving a trail of cursing in her wake. The trail led directly away from the inn where the rest of the party waited. She wished she had a way to contact them. Fights were Willow and G'herron's specialty.

The trail led to a decent-sized house. With a non-descript human standing lookout at the door. She perforated him with a Flying Sword of Light before he could pull a bell-rope. She charged the door.

It gave. Three humans surrounded Hur, who knelt next to a fourth lying on a fainting couch. Each of the humans had a hand on a weapon. Hur joined them in looking up at her entrance.

"Wil!" he exclaimed. "I was about to tell these gentlemen the good news." He looked at them. "Your friend has no curse upon him."

"Trap!" shouted Bruwilde. The humans drew weapons. Her Stroke of Lightning cut one attacker in half and shocked the rest into immobility.

"What?" she said. "Never seen a dwarf wizard before?" She stapled another human with a Sword of Light. The third rushed her before she could launch another spell.

* * *

"Please," said Hur. "Surrender before you are harmed." The human tried to stab him again with a dagger even as he went for a sword.

Hur grabbed the knife-wrist and squeezed. The dagger dropped as bones ground in his grip. A feeling of power surged in him. He let go instantly, but the human kept up the stupid.

In the background, Wil yelled in pain. Blood ran down her arm. Hur grabbed his mace off his belt. He had to end this quickly.

The human's sword did not stop the mace. And his head did little better. Hur hated the weapon for the power it gave him. And how it made him feel.

He noticed nothing as he strode across the room, winding up for another swing. Wil looked surprised when the human vanished from in front of her, replaced by Hur. The human hit a nearby wall and slumped, chest half caved in.

He wanted to charge over and pulp the human with his mace. His orcish blood bumed. He fought it down and knelt to tend Wil's wounds.

"You really need to learn to block better," he said. He hoped he kept the bloodthirsty growl suppressed. The peaceful prayer that would close her wounds was harder than pushing Mohg. She had been the last to give him grudging acceptance; now she was his best friend. Their shared interest in magic had helped. He still hoped to win her to the White from the Grey. Her wounds closed as his prayer was answered.

"More power and I would not have needed to," she said. "What possessed you to go with them?"

"They had a friend under a curse," he said.

Wil sighed. "Once again, your heart is bigger than your brain." She reached up and clapped him on the shoulder. "Your blessing and curse. Do not change. Come on. We should look around for clues. And money so Mohg will not complain."

"You go ahead. I will see if any of our attackers still live," he said.

She nodded and started searching. Hur checked each of the humans for signs of life. Wil's magic and his mace had been all too effective. He prayed about their passing.

Wil regarded the fallen as little more than rotten and messy meat. He prayed about her hard heart as well. She went through their pockets and pouches, grumbling about the absent Mohg.

"More pictures and instructions, but nothing about what to do with us," she said. "I think we will have to ask the dead."

Hur sighed. He wished again that he had never learned that prayer. Because it required the dead to work. He did not like being around the dead. He was no necromancer or priest of Mantor. Still, better to do it himself than encourage Wil to pursue that line of magic.

"Very well. Which one shall we question?"

"This one. He was obviously the leader. And his head is still intact." She pointed to the one halved by her lightning. At least she understood the restrictions on his magic. He needed brain, mouth, and lungs intact, and the dead could only testify about what they knew in life. He prayed.

Light enveloped the torso. It felt like he was trying to pick up G'herron. The magic was using his strength to animate the remains, for a time.

"Ask your questions," said the priest.

"What were you to do once you had the priest captured?"

"Bind him with steel shackles and take him to the southern downtrail," replied the human in a hollow voice. As it spoke, Hur struggled to breathe.

"What then?"

"We get paid, and try to catch another one."

"Is there a sign or signal?"

"There are sentries. There is no way to approach unseen."

"Let him go Hur. I think we are done here."

He released the magic with a sigh of relief. He felt lighter than Willow. He also had a realization.

"Perhaps we should go. I would hate to have some innocent guardsman caught up in this."

"Yes." They went out of the back of the house. From a pouch, Wil pulled a small bag and threw it inside. Fire bloomed.

"'Was that necessary?" he said.

"Distraction. I was tempted to use Fire Blossom, but restrained myself for your sake."

"Thank you." He knew the spell she was talking about. It would destroy the house and spread the fire for a long distance. Instead of a single house, and possibly a few neighbors, a large portion of the city would bum. Sometimes he wondered what would happen if he were not with them. Probably leave a trail of destruction a mile wide. With another prayer and a short gesture, the blood slid off their garments.

He endured the jeers and slights of passers-by on the way back to the inn. Responding with violence or even giving a reaction would only reinforce their prejudice. And the small rush of pleasure would not outweigh his disappointment with himself at his lack of discipline.

G'herron would understand. His training at the monastery gave him a discipline the orc envied. Willow always flew where her emotions blew. And

Mohg was lazy and selfish. Bruwilde fell somewhere in the middle; her main focus was on the acquisition of magic.

They found the others in the common room of the inn. All three looked disheveled and had straw sticking out of their hair.

"What happened to you?" said Wil.

Mohg took a drink. Willow giggled. And G'herron simply said, "A workman is worth his wages." Hur did not understand.

"What?" he said.

"I think the translation is: 'You owe me'," said Wil.

The centaur nodded and Willow collapsed off the stool in laughter. Hur reached down and covered her exposed body with her cloak. She only laughed harder. Wil took an empty seat.

"So, what did you two learn?" said Mohg.

"'We are up against a demon," said Wil. She paused to call the serving girl over and order ale.

"We already knew *that*," said the giant.

"A powerful demon named Tharwwar, that lives down in the Rift. We need to go take care of it."

"Great! Action! How do we kill it?" said Willow.

"You get to chop it to pieces with that ridiculous sword of yours," said the dwarf.

Willow nearly jumped out of her cloak with excitement; drawing looks from nearly every male in the room. Bruwilde shook her head. Hur looked away, embarrassed. He was rather glad her flirtations with him were minimal; he did not want to harm her. Elves were so fragile.

"Do not forget to tell them about the sentries," he said.

"I was getting to that," said Wil. "First things first. The demon's preferred weapon is a sword rimed with frost, and it can throw off waves of cold as well. I figure Hur and I can keep it from freezing us."

"I hope at least one of the guys will help me warm up afterwards," said Willow.

"What about me and G'herron?" said Mohg.

"You two get to take out the sentries. We were told there is no way past them to the downtrail."

Hur nodded. He was glad they had Bruwilde for research and planning. She was the smartest of them. Then he remembered something.

"Oh, I managed to identify the potions. Before I got led into that trap."

"Trap?" said Mohg.

* * *

He took another drink of his water as the story

wound down. yet another episode of the orc thinking with his heart. A good heart unmatched by any G'herron had met so far. Even the monks of Sunspire Keep.

His form had posed a unique challenge to the monks for his training. Training ended the day Worfess stamped him with the Mark of the Gods. And now, over a cycle later, he traveled with the most chaotic, undisciplined, frustrating, and effective heroes he could think of.

"A straight staff reaches farther than a tangle of branches," he said, interrupting. It was time to bring them back to the problem at hand.

"G'herron is right," said Willow. "Less talk, more action."

"I think he meant for us to get back to the task at hand," said Bruwilde. The centaur was pleased. Usually it was Hur that understood him best.

While the conversation went back to planning, he practiced his breathing. He isolated and stretched each muscle group without the rest of them noticing. He lived a life of discipline. He was always ready.

Soon it was time to go. He and Mohg set off toward the trail that descended into the Rift. The others would follow. Over a mile deep and a thousand miles north and south of the bridge between East- and Westtower, it was known to be full of demons, monsters, and other terrors. Hence the prosperity of the trade cities. And his friends were going right into it.

The sun was setting, and the first of the three moons was rising. They paralleled the edge of the Rift out about a quarter-mile. About a mile from the trailhead, he separated from Mohg. The giant carried a tree to use as a disguise. G'herron went to the edge of the chasm.

The rock was broken, providing plenty of holds. Here and there, a hardy tree or bush thrust out of a cleft. Goats and monkeys would not stand a chance. Compared to the training cliff by Sunspire Keep, it was a novice's exercise. Five hundred feet down, he saw a trail clinging to the Rift wall.

It was all a matter of balance. Even though he weighed over a ton, he leapt and skipped down the cliff lighter than dandelion fluff. He still remembered the disbelief on his friends' faces when he galloped across the surface of a pond.

As easy as walking on flat ground, he finished his descent. In shadow from the setting sun, he looked around for signs of trouble. The trail showed only occasional use by small numbers of humanoids. He started uphill.

Both sets of lungs pumped easily as he climbed.

His ears flicked as he listened for movement. If he were surprised, his companions would never let him hear the end of it. The signs of use on the trail increased.

The creak of leather and clink of metal caught his attention. He rounded an outcrop and ran into a pair of sentries standing outside a cave. Human sentries. G'herron moved.

He drove his palm into the chest of the one on the right. His foreshoulder sent the one on his left sailing into the abyss. He caught the dead sentry and sent him after his companion. The tracks continuing up the trail increased.

The interior of the cave was dark, and he heard no movement. He continued uphill. At regular intervals, he surprised and overwhelmed pairs of sentries. Obviously they expected no trouble from below. At the top, just before the crest, he ran into a real fight.

There were four of them, and one had the insight to watch the backtrail. G'herron did not waste time cursing. He slapped aside the first man's sword and sent him plummeting.

The next two came together, one attacking high, the other going low for his legs. G'herron reared, lashing out with his forehooves. A blade grazed his skin, turned by his Iron Skin technique. His kick felled the lead human. The fourth aimed a crossbow.

G'herron dodged a couple more attacks from the swordsman as he watched the archer. This one was smart, aiming for his equine barrel. When his eyes narrowed and his fingers tightened, G'herron blurred his hand and caught the bolt.

The sword scored a line of blood on his abdomen. He ignored the pain. His world shrank to encompass only the present conflict. No worry for the future. No looking at the past. Only the now.

The last swordsman fought defensively while the archer blew a whistle as he reloaded. G'herron ignored the stinging nicks on his forearms. Then the opening occurred.

The swordsman lunged. The centaur moved aside, caught the sword-hand, and launched him off the trail. He screamed all the way down. Now only the archer remained. He slipped the bolt and raised the crossbow.

And vanished in a wall of moving green. The bolt skipped off the trail near the centaur's hooves. The tree went over the side, taking the archer with it. Mohg grinned from the rim of the canyon. The fight was over.

G'herron took a deep double-breath and

performed a cool-down exercise. Mohg waved up the others to join them.

"Good idea, whistling to signal me," said the giant.

"A good watchman sounds the alarm," said the centaur. "But the better one takes away any who would answer."

"Lucky for us then," said the giant. G'herron was sure he was only playing along and did not understand. The giant removed the pouches of the fallen swordsman before tossing the body over the side. Then he rooted through the guardhouse, and came out with a pot of stew. "Want some?"

The centaur simply shook his head.

"Suit yourself." He downed the entire pot in a matter of seconds. G'herron shook his head again at the giant's gluttony. The rest of his companions joined them.

Hur stepped forward and healed G'herron's wounds. The centaur nodded his thanks. He had learned that refusing healing was prideful and foolish. Bruwilde looked over the edge. Willow was already naked, massive blade in hand. She looked around for something to kill.

"You did not save any for me?" she pouted.

* * *

The centaur just looked at her. Willow figured he did not have some mystical proverb for an answer. Centaurs were *supposed* to be drunkards and hedonists to put Mohg to shame. Just her luck to find the exception.

At least he could fight, though he had no more concept of honor than Mohg. Hur was far more kind and noble than any, but so *ugly*. If only his face were as beautiful as his soul. And Bruwilde was just plain *scary*, so driven to gain mystical power that she dressed as a male just to avoid distractions.

"Hey doll," said Mohg. At least *he* noticed she was female. "Ready to chop a big bad demon into little quivering bits?"

"I did not get undressed for nothing." She started down the trail. A blessing received just before Worfess marked her prevented any weapon from breaking her skin, so long as she was clad only in the sky. He had given her the Starblade himself.

If not for the magic that bonded it to her soul, she would be as unable to wield the gigantic blade as an infant. It was the only weapon they had that could harm the demon. The rest of her group fell in behind her.

The wind caressed her bare skin as she jogged down the trail. At least it was a warm wind. She did not look forward to fighting naked in sub-freezing cold. At least the males would get a good show.

They reached the cave entrance with no problems. She stepped inside, the Starblade glowing brighter than any lightstone. The cave was easily large enough to admit both centaur and giant. Not the best sign. Large demons could hit hard. Just because her skin could not be pierced, did not mean she was invulnerable. Just mostly.

A short distance inside, the cave ended abruptly. She waved Mohg forward. Up close, she could feel his warmth.

"Time to check for secret doors, eh?" he said. From a pouch, he pulled a small anvil. The noise as he bashed it against the rock hurt her ears. A few minutes later, he found the door; by breaking a hole in it, followed by kicking it down. Cold blasted out of the opening.

"Good," she said. "Now they know we are coming. We will not have long to wait now." She strode forward, Starblade ready.

The main tunnel wound into the rock, occasionally opening into smaller side passages. G'herron dropped back to be rearguard. Nothing would get past him. The centaur was focus embodied; she just wished he would loosen up a bit.

She almost missed the ambush. Four fur-clad humans burst out of a side passage, swords bared. She warded them away with her sword, chopping through two of their weapons. Their eyes widened as they took in her naked form.

"Surrender boys. I want some prisoners," she said. They did not surrender. Instead, they attacked. The Starblade left only pieces. She continued her advance.

"Wait," said Mohg. "I think there may be a trap around." She stopped.

"Why?" said Wil.

"Because they came from the side. And I would put one just past an ambush."

"Good point," said Wil.

"Why bother? I can live through any trap," said Willow.

"Want to bet?" He pulled a round rock from his pouch and rolled it down the tunnel. A rock that likely weighed as much as she did.

It vanished forty feet down the hall in a puff of dust. Willow paled. Poison would kill her easily. They moved ahead slowly. The giant took a waterskin and sluiced the ground ahead.

And pointed out the area supported by trapdoors. Once identified, the trapdoors were easily jumped by all but the dwarf. G'herron tossed her to Mohg. The dwarf had long since ceased complaining. Willow continued to lead the way. Finally, they reached a pair of massive metal doors. Cold poured off them in waves.

"Mohg, would you please open the door?" said Willow, trying not to shiver. "Quickly?"

He used his anvil-shaped key to break them open. Bitter cold rolled out. Willow felt her skin prickle. A red bead streaked past her and bloomed into a ball of flame in the massive cavern; Bruwilde's Fire Blossom.

Willow spotted the demon in the fiery flash. Along with plenty of minions in heavy furs. It stood half-again the height of Mohg; over three times her own. Its, his—obviously his—skin ranged from ice-blue to frost-white. And it was uglier than Hur.

"Surrender and I will let all of you, except the demon, live!" shouted Willow.

"Subdue them all! And bring the wench to me!" howled the demon. Willow charged, honor was satisfied.

Her bare feet slid on the wet stone. A pair of humans barred her way for only a moment. She never broke stride as she cut them down. A bolt of white frost from the demon met a silvery-white beam from behind her. Hur's countermagic.

The clash of fighting rang behind Willow. She ignored it. Whatever the others thought, she could focus as well as anyone. She had a demon to fight.

As she closed, the briefly-warmed air went cold. The demon produced a sword as large as her Starblade. She met its swing and deflected it in a shower of sparks. Her feet were numb.

The demon opened its mouth to speak. She attacked each time it tried to talk. She had no interest in anything it had to say. It would be boastful drivel anyway.

The elf started slowing. Just being close to the demon and its blade was killing her. The demon made playful feints at her.

A warm bteeze washed over her. Hur suddenly appeared next to her, glowing like the sun and holding a mace of light. The demon blocked Hur's clumsy swings and slashed him across the chest.

Willow used the opening to cut the demon off at the knees. How dare he harm Hur. The orc fell to one knee, glow fading. The light had turned the worst of the blow.

The demon screamed as it fell, losing parts to her Starblade as she could reach them. It felt like plunging into icy water with each swing. Willow gasped for air.

Silence fell. Hur stood next to her, pity on his face even for the demon. Willow turned to look at the rest of the battlefield.

Bruwilde sat on a fallen human, blood trickling down her scalp. Mohg was already 'picking pockets.' G'herron, bleeding from a dozen minor wounds, did some weird stretching and breathing exercise.

"Hur," said Willow before he could leave her side. "Want to help me warm up?"

He smiled and pulled her cloak from his pack. He flung it around her shoulders and prayed it warm.

"That is not what I meant."

"I know." He went to heal the wounds of the others.

Willow looked down at her Starblade. It slowly faded away, ready to appear in an instant at her need. The battle was over, and she felt empty again.

Everyone else had something to do in the aftermath. Mohg collected the loot. Bruwilde studied, looking for clues and information. Hur tended wounds and prayed for the dead.

"True battle is within, not without," said the centaur. He was there to keep her from looking for more trouble.

She jumped up on his equine back. He bore her with stoic dignity. She lay back-to-back, feet dangling off either side, soaking up his warmth.

"When we get back to Westtower, I am so getting laid," she said. She wondered why the others, save Mohg, cared so little about pleasure.

"Each seek their pleasure in different ways," said the centaur.

"I could teach you a few things."

The centaur only chuckled and walked slowly around the room. Willow watched the others as they worked. Maybe she should learn to do more than just fight? Fighting was what she did for the group, her role. If not for her, they would have died several times over. With the demon dead, the room slowly warmed.

She was approaching sleepy boredom when the others finished. She slid off G'herron's back when it was time to leave. When they reached the lip of the Rift, it was deep dark. She doffed her cloak as they approached the city. Time for her other job.

She ran ahead of the party, pale skin glowing in the moonlight. She could feel eyes drawn to her.

"The gate! Please open the gate!" she cried as

she approached. Twenty paces out, the creaking and groaning began. At ten, light spilled through the open doors.

"Inside. Quickly," said a human guard.

She stopped just in the gateway, chest heaving. The guard stared. She leaned on the gate.

"Thank you," panted Willow. The guard kept staring.

"Hurry and get her inside," hissed a voice from above.

A huge hand caught the gate over her head. The rest of the party had arrived.

"Thank you for opening the gate for us," said Mohg.

Willow slipped through the opening, followed by the others. The guard looked sick. Willow sidled up to him and put her arms around his neck. Up close, he was decent looking, for a human.

"We promise not to tell anyone," she breathed in his ear. "And I would like to personally thank you." His tremble was all the reply she needed.

"Go ahead friends," she told her companions. "I will join you after I take care of our gate fees…"

* * *

"When Worfess chooses Heroes, sometimes he chooses the most unlikely combinations. Always for a reason. It reminds me of one of my own adventures. But that is another story…"

Daybreak

South by southeast
along the curve of the world
sailed the demon's ship
back to his fortress.

Behind the ship,
dawn spread over
the burnt towns—
Angshan, Jozhou, Aldford,
Lare, Harmouth, Polton—
the third dawn
since the demon's death.

South by southeast
sailed the demon's crew,
bringing the king
who slew the demon,
the king who saved them
from the demon's spell,
King Xau, who stared down
at the heaving ocean
into which he heaved,
miserably, his breakfast.

Swiftly they closed on
the demon's fortress,
day already bright
on its battlements.
Within, the demon's servants
—unbound, undone by his undoing—
lay, parched, on the stones,
the men, women, children
who had knelt to the demon
as he burnt their towns
(Polton, Harmouth, Lare,
Aldford, Jozhou, Angshan).

To save them, the sailors
brought the king,
the king who would
call them home.

— Mary Soon Lee

Flyover

Story by
Frank Tavares

Illustration by
Tom Kelly

It's a beautiful day for flying. Just below the treetops on the busy city block. People watching me in amazement.

I don't recall flying before. Perhaps I never tried. Never realized I could. Spread my arms, close my eyes, let go.

There's my friend Oswald heading into the office. "Ozzzz!" I yell. He sees me, but doesn't wave. He's just standing there, frozen, mouth open. If I wasn't quite so high, I'd reach down and snap that Styrofoam cup out of his hand. Probably not a good idea, but it'd get a laugh.

Over a city bus right now. Number 3-4-4-3. Numbers written large on top. I've only seen them in photos. Makes it easy to identify from the air.

There's Juliette. Mid stride. She left for the office before me this morning. She's on her cell phone. We make sure no one sees us coming or going together. There's no policy about sleeping with co-workers, but neither of us needs the grief. Besides, she's still married. They're getting a divorce, but some of our colleagues would frown on it. We're very careful. Her ex-to-be works here, too. In security on the ground floor. Sometimes he mans the desk in the lobby. All Juliette needs is for him to see us coming in together laughing or touching. Or catch us on an elevator monitor groping one another. She'd end up paying his mortgage. She rented a small studio only half a dozen blocks east. An easy walk to work. But she's been staying most nights at my place. Less convenient, but I've got more room. Not that we need it. When she's over we hardly leave the bed. It's been a great couple of weeks.

I love watching her walk. The heels set off her calves and tighten her rear. Love it. Hard to see from up here, but I can almost feel it.

I'm rolling now. Trick flying. Who knew! I can look up at the tops of the buildings on the block. Ours is a six story box, steel and glass. It's facing east and catches the morning sun. Hadn't noticed before how it reflects the rays into its twin across the street. You can see right into the offices. If I turn just right, I'll be able to catch myself in the reflection.

There I am! Flying. Arms flailing. Tie askew. I don't look very happy. My mouth is open. There's my briefcase, just below me. It's open, too; contents leaving a paper contrail.

For such a busy morning, it's quiet. I can't hear the traffic on the street below. Or the people on the sidewalk. Several of them have turned and are watching me. They're frozen, too. Eyes wide, mouths open. I wish I had a camera. My cell phone. I could take a picture with my cell phone. It's open in my hand. I was talking to someone.

I *have* flown before. I remember now. When I was a boy. Playing with my best friend Jimmy. We had climbed on the roof of my daddy's barn. I lost my footing and slid the length of its slope. When I got to the edge I pushed off as if diving into a pool and flew. Peaceful. Quiet. Like now. Don't remember landing. My dad was upset, but not angry. Tight lipped by my hospital bed. How'd I get here from there?

I'm landing now. Coming down in front of a cab. Don't think the driver sees me. I'll land right in front of him. Maybe on him. On his hood. On his windshield. I need to tuck my head.

* * *

"An unfortunate death this morning in midtown. A thirty-four year old pedestrian on his way to work was struck and killed by a truck that apparently ran a light. The victim, whose name is being withheld pending notification of next-of-kin, was less than a block from his office when hit. Witnesses said the impact was so strong, it actually sent him flying over a city bus and into the windshield of an oncoming taxi. The driver of the cab sustained minor injuries from flying glass, and was treated and released from a local hospital. The driver of the truck was unhurt and cited for excessive speed, erratic driving, and failure to obey a traffic control device. Ironically, the driver was an employee working in security at the same company where the victim worked. More news, weather, and Mort-with-the-Sports, right after the break."

Mountain

I did this on my own.
First memories:
a humble pebble, but ambitious,
rolling, growing
by dint of stonework,
stonewalling,
rock-hard determination,
cobbled myself together—
ah, bouldery youth!

Eventually, we all stop rolling, eh?
Some slide, are buried and forgot,
some peak early.
I created myself
AND my own weather shadow climate,
metaphor Myself, my name is all,
stand tall, exhort my foothills:
grow you to almost me!

It's said we begin as sand, or silt,
dumb rocks and nothing more,
I don't call this blasphemy,
but reason tells me it ain't so,
silt's mud but for the grace of sieve,
sand's little more: shells are bigger;
so rock on, sand, if rock you be,
but never think that rock is Me.

About our hot-tempered "brethren"
the less said the better,
we are not close, not in that way,
I am not descended from a bit
of fiery stuff, obscenely quenched,
no more from lights glimmering in darkness.

When I've grown enough to free myself
of this thinning air you'll see
what it means to Me;
oh! scuse my landslide, that quake's
not mine, it came from Terra Incognita's
bowels, and not from me.

— David C. Kopaska-Merkel

Gypsy

I entered the Gypsy's tent
A Fortune Teller's dwelling
Swirling, heady scents
Their perfume was foretelling

Purple folds cascaded
From the tented peaks
Reality soon faded
The sensual so sweet

The divinatory beckoned
I sat down at the table
She seemed to start sensing
An energy unstable

She lit a scarlet candle
Had me stare into the orb
I did as she would bid
Expecting to be awed

I gazed into the glassy sphere
Looking long and deep
Would I find my future here?
The answers I did seek

I searched and scanned that magic space
I could not find what lay ahead
Reflected there was my own face
No secret message to be read

The wise old gypsy looked at me
And she simply said
"All the magic that you need
Is conjured in your head"

— Louise Webster

Dear Cthulhu

by
Patrick Thomas

Dear Cthulhu,

I'm a woman who lives in a big city. I just moved here for a job and I haven't made many friends yet. I'm just out of college and I don't make a lot of money, so I have to take the subway to work every day. I didn't used to mind, but recently something has changed.

There's a guy who's been bothering me on the train. I thought it was weird how he always seemed to end up standing next to me. I don't know many people in the city so I figured I'd say hi, maybe strike up a conversation and meet someone new. I thought he must have been shyer than me because he barely managed to whisper hi and the conversation didn't progress past that. As the week went on he started standing closer to me, rubbing up against my back or my front. In a crowded subway car at rush-hour that's not too uncommon so didn't think too much of it until one day when I felt his hand grab my butt. I was so shocked I froze and things got worse as he kept doing it. I tried to move away from him, but he followed me.

I started taking trains at different times, but he always seemed to get on my train and on the same car. It progressed to the point where he started grinding against me. I was afraid and ashamed so I just stood there and tried to ignore it as best I could. I looked around at the other passengers hoping to find someone to help me, but they were all too busy reading the paper or texting or talking on their phones to notice what was happening to me, so I stood there and did my best to ignore it until my subway stop came.

For the first time, he got off at my stop. I sprinted up the stairs and down the street and he didn't follow.

That was Thursday. I called in sick to work on Friday but I'm really worried about what's going to happen on Monday. The buses don't go anywhere near work. I can't afford a cab and it's too far to walk.

What should I do?

— Frightened On The Subway

Dear Frightened,

The first and best thing Cthulhu can recommend to you is to cease being a victim. No other human has the right to touch or otherwise assault you against your will. It is one of the rights Cthulhu grants you. This lowlife predator got bolder because you ignored his first assaults.

There are several ways to handle this. You could report him to your local police force. The truth of it however is most police departments are understaffed and overworked. Without any other witnesses, it would be your word against his. Unfortunately for you, the criminal justice system in your country is still often skewed and tries to place some blame on the woman for these kind of assaults. And oddly many of these same people who do this would consider Cthulhu evil.

You might be able to get an order of protection, but the value of that is limited by how well the predator follows it. Of course the police could do an undercover sting operation, but the odds of them doing that for what *they* would consider a simple groping are minimal. You stand a better chance of winning a lottery.

Do you have a group of friends or co-worker who could ride with you? There can be safety in numbers.

This predator appears to be counting on you being too embarrassed to do anything to stop him. Turn the tables. The next time he tries to assault you, be loud and make a scene. Bring attention to what he is doing. Embarrass him. Yell things like "Why is your hand on my buttocks?" or "Why are you grinding up against me?" Loudly demand that he stop. Do not be embarrassed as you have done nothing wrong. All fault is his.

Film him with your cellphone. Suggest others riding with you do the same. Although from his chosen method of attack he appears to be a coward, there is no guarantee that he will not resort to violence, so do not do anything you do not think you can handle.

Of course, even if this makes him go away, this poor excuse for a human may still prey on other women. A moment of embarrassment is hardly a real punishment for his assaults on your person and the fear he caused you. In an ideal world, the only one you should fear is Cthulhu himself. Alas, you humans prevent this world from being ideal.

The preferred option of Cthulhu is to punish the wrong doer and to enjoy one's self when doing it. Purchase a handheld stun gun. Like many dangerous things, they are available on the internet. It is powered by a nine-volt battery. When you return to the subway, pull your hand up into the sleeve of your coat and hide the stun gun. When this poor excuse for a human starts his attack on your person, place the stun gun up against him—perhaps even the same area he is grinding against you—and press the button. Repeatedly. This will likely knock him to his knees, so it would be best to wait until you are near a subway stop. Do it just before the train halts and then get off. That way you are less likely to be caught by law enforcement for defending yourself. If you are caught, tell them the truth about what has been happening, making sure to weep and sob. This will likely help your case as humans seem to feel worse for their fellow humans that do this. With luck, you will be let off with a warning. Or if filmed by your fellow passengers, become a viral sensation for a being a female bold enough to put a predatory male down in his place.

At the very least, this poor excuse for a human will likely reconsider assaulting any more women.

Dear Cthulhu,

I started at my company five years ago—believe it or not—in the mailroom. I was never popular in high school or college and learned to get by without people. I mean I have family and they're okay. At least I can tolerate them in small doses around the holidays.

Because of my lack of a social life, I really don't have much problem working 80 hours a week, which helps explain how I became the youngest vice president in my company's history. Of course, sometimes I was lonely but I have lots of money and was able to buy companionship, if you know what I mean.

My sister was worried about me and for my birthday bought me a puppy. At first I thought it was a horrible gift. I was going to take it to an animal shelter the next day, but then the little guy climbed up into my lap and licked my face. I started to pet him. I fell asleep with the dog next to me and by the next morning I decided to keep "Runt".

Over the next few weeks, a strange thing happened. I had more to look forward to than just work. I actually stopped going into the office on weekends. I left work by 8 o'clock instead of 10, so I'd have time to go home and take Runt for a walk, then play with him before going to bed. I hired a dog walker to take him out while I was at work.

I finally had something that money couldn't buy, love and companionship. Not that there's anything freaky between me and the dog. Well, there was that one night that I came home drunk and woke up with peanut butter in embarrassing places, but that's something the dog and I are doing our best to pretend never happened.

All was well until my dog walker went off and joined the Occupy The Coffee Party movement. That meant I had to hire another one. I picked the nicest one with the best references, which may have been the biggest mistake of my life. It was a senior citizen who was living on her pension and looking for some supplemental income. Apparently she had too much time on her hands and decided to spend most of it with my dog. Instead of just walking him, she took him out to play for hours at the dog park. She cooked him homemade meals and knitted him sweaters. Now Runt seems happier to see the old lady then he does me. By the time I get home from work he's too tired to go for a long walk and he barely wants to play.

What it boils down to is I think my dog loves his dog walker more than he does me. And it's driving me crazy. Am I just being paranoid? Would it be wrong of me to set some boundaries about what she can and cannot do with my dog? A dog is supposed to love its owner more than anybody else right? Isn't that a rule or a law or something?

I met a guy at a conference who claims he knows people that will knock off somebody else for a few grand. Would it be wrong of me to put a hit out on this woman so I have my dog all to myself again?

— Aggravated Doggie Daddy in Denver

Dear Denver,

No, you are not being paranoid. Cthulhu gets a multitude of letters from people whose loved ones' affection has been alienated from them and given to another. True, usually it is a spouse or significant other, but the principle is the same. I also get letters from the people who do the moving on. They tell me about how their former loved one doesn't spend time with them anymore. One of the more common reasons is because they are too busy with work. Most of these people tell Cthulhu that the person that they cheat with is not necessarily better looking or more skilled at procreation. It is simply a matter of them being willing to spend time with them and lavish them with at least the illusion of affection. It is important for most humans to feel as though somebody cares about them.

The same appears to have happened with you and your dog. By your own admission, even though you have cut down the amount of hours you spend earning a living, you still devote the majority of your time to your job while this woman spends most of hers with the canine. It is only natural that the pair would form a bond. And since she spends more time, it stands to reason their bond would be stronger.

As to whether or not you should hire others to end the woman's life, Cthulhu says no. Cthulhu's position on humans killing other humans remains unchanged. All humanity will one day be the property of Cthulhu and no one other than Cthulhu has the right to destroy Cthulhu's property.

There is a much easier solution that you are overlooking. Simply fire the woman and hire another dog walker, preferably a professional who has a number of clients whose dogs get walked at the same time. This ensures that your dog gets some socialization with other of its kind, but that neither he nor the dog walker will get overly attached to each other.

Then you can slowly begin the task of rebuilding a relationship with your canine. You mentioned working many hours, but you do not mention anything about taking vacations. There are places that will cater to holidays specifically for people and their pets. Look into one and take some time off and go. Then once a month, take a day or half a day off and come home to spend time with your dog. Look in to the option of telecommuting. Are there any of your duties that could be done from home? If this is possible you would be able to work and be with the dog at the same time.

If this does not work and your dog refuses to return your affections to your satisfaction, remember the dog is a lower life form as compared to you, much like humans are to Cthulhu. That gives you the right to decide whether it lives or dies. And if you decide to end its existence, might Cthulhu recommend doing so by way of barbecue. While not as tasty as kitten, dog roasted on a spit with some rosemary and sage can be quite a delicacy. Then you can simply get another dog and start over. Or—because PETA will be upset with my last recommendation—you could consider gifting the dog to the old woman and simply getting a new one for yourself. Or if you decide to go with the first option, invite the old woman over for

a barbecue dinner. I doubt she will be bonding with anyone else's pet after that.

Have A Dark Day.

LEGEND & SHOOTIST

Story by D.J. Tyrer
Illustration by Paul Niemiec

Archer was a marshal with a shotgun in his arm and a devil in his chest and he was on the trail of the gunman known as Legend and Shootist. It was thanks to Legend and Shootist that his left arm had been replaced with one of struts and springs powered by the turn of a key. The devil was very much his own fault. So, the hunt was as much personal for him as it was his duty. The fingers of his left hand flexed with a soft whirr and click at the thought of finally having his showdown.

He surveyed the trail ahead, the targeting lens that replaced his left eye automatically focusing at the twitch of the muscle; that rebuild was another legacy of his encounter with his quarry. A bullet from Legend and Shootist's gun had blown a chunk from his skull and taken his eye with it; the wound had been rebuilt with copper and bronze and a special lens that had improved his aim tenfold. Archer almost considered the loss of his eye worthwhile for the benefits that the repair had provided.

Spurring his mount, Jaxon, Archer set off down the trail. The distinctive right-angle shoeprints of his quarry's horse were visible still—he was probably no more than a day or two behind him. It was almost as if the weasel was taunting him, wanted him to follow him so that he could finish the job—that was what he'd expect of the gunman's hubris. Legend and Shootist would never worry that he might be endangered. That was what Archer was hoping, anyway, that his prey's overconfidence meant he would blunder into his sights. He just had to hope that that confidence wasn't justified and that it would be him who would find himself in the other's aim. He thought that the changes since last they'd met meant they were on an equal footing and, now, he knew—knew all too well—what his enemy was capable of.

Legend and Shootist was not a normal man. He was no more normal than Archer now was. He was not even a single man, not as such: although the name by which he was known throughout the Territories was due to his skill as a gunman or shootist and the fact that he was one of the legends of the West, it also indicated a salient fact: somehow, the outlaw was capable of splitting himself in two; Legend and Shootist were two aspects of one being. That was how he'd got the drop on Archer: he'd chased after his quarry and had seen him disappear through a doorway only to spot him moving through a nearby alleyway; following the movement, he'd turned only for the other to reappear through the doorway and plug him twice. As he'd lain bleeding in the dust,

thinking he was dying, he'd been amazed to see the two versions of the outlaw merge into a single figure. He would not be caught like that this time. Legend and Shootist was going to die.

He spotted smoke rising from beyond a scrubby ridge and dismounted and tied Jaxon to a stump. He wanted to scout out what lay ahead before he just went riding in. Creeping his way up the ridge and keeping low, Archer surveyed what proved to be a small town. Was the outlaw hiding out somewhere in the town, or perhaps living it up in the saloon or cathouse? Or, had he passed through already, headed somewhere else or maybe fleeing the aftermath of some new criminal outrage? There was only one way to find out.

Archer kept glancing about him as he rode into town. A neatly-painted sign said 'Welcome to Norrisville'. It seemed quiet. His good eye was good enough, but his replacement one acted as a magnifier of sorts, so he was pretty confident he would spot any varmints in his vicinity. There didn't appear to be any.

Then, he heard the screams and the shrieked protestations of "I'm not that sorta woman! Get your hands off me!"

He could guess what was happening; it was an all-too-common story in these parts where women were rarer than gold and buffalo skins. Men who'd got used to taking what they wanted from nature began to believe they could take what they wanted from women just as easily. The presence of cathouses in almost every town only served to inflame the situation rather than sate the men's appetites, as they only served to give the impression that every girl 'gone out west' was willing to provide a service. Some men just seemed incapable of understanding that such impressions were wrong.

He spurred his horse in the direction of the cries and Jaxon cantered obediently through the town. Archer would take a certain pleasure in disabusing the man of his error.

Turning a corner, he confronted the scene of a young woman in a purple dress and matching bonnet being pursued by a man in grey-brown long-johns, a broken whisky bottle on the ground nearby. The man held a large Bowie knife in his right hand and the torn-off sleeve of the woman's dress in his left. Had it not been for that vicious and unpleasantly-stained knife, Archer had the suspicion that the woman wouldn't have been anywhere as terrified as she was and would have easily fended off his unwanted attentions.

"Hoi!" he shouted. "Leave her be!"

As a marshal, he was well-versed in bellowing orders at miscreants and wasn't surprised that the man turned at his barked order. Unfortunately, the man was drunk enough to neither notice nor care who shouted at him and belligerently replied in exceptionally colorful and rather incoherent language that Archer ought to mind his own business for the good of his health. He waved the knife at him to emphasise the point.

"Put the knife down, son. I'm a Federal Marshal and I'm ordering you to put the weapon down."

The man just cussed him and came at him with the knife.

Archer sighed with irritation and drew his revolver with his right hand, almost casually—he saw no point in wasting a shot shell and the hassle of reloading his arm on him—and took careful aim, using his targeter to pinpoint the blade of the knife. He squeezed the trigger and sent the weapon flying from the man's hand.

The man looked stupidly down at his empty hand then up at Archer.

Suddenly, his eyes widened, a dribble of blood escaped his lips and ran down his chin, and he collapsed to his knees, before falling face down in the dust of the yard. The woman stood over him, the bloodied neck of the broken bottle in her hand. There were three or four bloody gashes in the man's back and he looked pretty dead.

"There was no need to kill him," Archer commented. The pathetic drunk hadn't, in his opinion, been worth killing.

"Yes, there was," she retorted, darkly, tossing the bottle neck aside. "Yes, there was." From her expression, it was clear this was not a point she was going to debate and he supposed only she knew the truth of it. Certainly, the man had brought it on himself.

He gave a slight shrug before holstering his gun.

"Thank you," said the woman, retrieving her sleeve. "This was my best dress…" she sighed. "I suppose it'll mend."

"You're welcome, Miss…"

"Mrs. Hannigan. Arlene Hannigan. Widow."

Well, that explained why the man had thought he could go for her. He either didn't really know her or was unobservant as a blind racoon if he hadn't realized what sort of woman he was dealing with.

"Pleased to meet you, ma'am. I'm Marshal Archer and I'm on the hunt for the notorious outlaw known as Legend and Shootist. I believe he came this way…"

"That dastard sure did come this way," she told him and he was surprised to see her stern features quiver just a little and the sheen of tears appear in her eyes. "That low-down, no-good, scum-sucking son-of-a-lame-coyote," she put venom into the words that most ranch hands were capable of investing the vilest of cuss-words with, "rode into town a couple of days back and announced himself as if he were some kind of gosh-darned celebrity, before shooting the sheriff dead." A sob escaped her lips. "My husband, Sheriff Evan Hannigan. Gunned him down like he were nought but a cur and laughed as he did it. The … the … devil! Laughed!"

"I'm sorry to hear that, ma'am. I plan on killing the fiend, and your story only firms up my conviction. Do you know which way the varmint went?"

"I surely do, sir. But, I won't be telling you…"

"Sorry?"

"I'll be showing you—or, I'll be pursuing him alone. I want to see that dastard dead, and how!"

He could believe that, but doubted she had the ability to deal with him, even if she had the gumption, and hated the idea of having her tag along with him, needing protection, and told her so.

"Don't talk to me as if I were a child, sir!" she responded, hotly. "I am a grown woman and I know how to handle a gun." She must have caught the question in his eye, as she told him: "That was where I was done going, to fetch a gun, when this … trash attacked me. My husband only ever let me have a little lady's gun, even though my pappy done taught me to fire a Winchester and a Corpsemaker when I were little. The guns in his office, though, to which I have the key, are up to the job."

He sighed. "Fine. Let's go fetch you a gun, then get after Legend and Shootist…"

She walked over to the back door of a nearby building, unlocked it and went inside, returning a couple of minutes later with a chunky Colt Corpsemaker holstered on her hip and a Winchester slung over her shoulder; she paused to strap a slim dagger to her thigh, then went over to a livery stable on the opposite side of the yard and led out a grey mare.

"Ready?" she asked, having mounted up and slipped the rifle into a saddle holster.

He nodded and went to fetch Jaxon.

"Follow me," she said when he returned. She trotted her mount out of the yard and through the town. Although there were the distant sound of gunshots and the raucous sounds of violence from the saloon, as one might expect to hear in a town without a sheriff, they encountered no trouble and were soon riding along a dirt track between plots of corn and beans, the town's concession to the necessity of survival. There weren't many of the little fields and soon they were riding across grassy scrub towards a shallow river, splashing through its chill waters to continue the pursuit on the far side, through a shadowy pine forest.

"I don't much like this place," she admitted over her shoulder as she rode ahead, leading the way. "It's dark and there's not much undergrowth—it feels dead. They say the woods are full of werewolves and devils."

"Such things are usually exaggeration," he told her, not caring to mention that she had been in the company of a devil for some time. The death of the man had roused the one in his chest from its half-slumber and it had purred with a sanguinary delight. It lusted after death and corruption. It wanted him to kill. The devil would have been delighted if only he would kill Arlene and perhaps ravish her into the bargain. It took a strong will to resist its primal urgings.

Of course, in his career, he had come to learn, the hard way, that such things as werewolves were seldom as exaggerated as one might wish and so Arlene's story proved. They had been riding through the woods for maybe half an hour when a rifle shot cracked and the bark of a nearby tree splintered. Perhaps the shot was intended as a warning, perhaps the unseen shooter was merely a bad shot, but Archer was taking no chances: he hurled himself off Jaxon's back and rolled into a crouch in the shelter of a pine, calling for Arlene to do likewise. Pausing only to wind the key in his left arm, he drew his gun with his right.

Arlene dismounted in alarm if with a little less alacrity as another gunshot cracked and pine needles not far from their mounts were kicked up by the shot. She copied his use of a trunk for cover and leveled the Winchester that she had managed to retrieve as she dismounted.

They peered through the gloom beneath the pines, attempting to discern who'd shot at them, but could see nobody. A third shot cracked and struck the tree behind which Arlene sheltered. They each opened fire at the approximate source of the shot, firing a couple of shots each to no apparent effect, then saw movement.

"I see three—no, four—of them," he whispered to her, not wanting them to hear how much—or how little—they'd noticed. She nodded a reply.

"Federal Marshal!" he called out, winding the key in his left arm a little further as he did so.

He received a gunshot in reply.

"I don't think they're friendly," Arlene muttered.

"Shoot 'em!" he snapped at her and they both took aim.

She wasn't a bad shot with the Winchester and he saw one of the figures go down before she needed to pause to reload. Even with his targeter-eye, his revolver was at the limit of its effective range and the wickerwork of pine trees made it difficult to get a clear shot; one figure seemed to stagger when a bullet surely hit his shoulder and another did fall. One of the figures carried a rifle and returned fire, thankfully inaccurately, but the others seemed unarmed. The devil in his chest was purring strongly now.

"Two down!" he hissed across to her as they reloaded. Then, his heart sank as the two they had thought shot stood and resumed their advance; they must have ducked for cover rather than been hit.

Now, the quartet was closer, and they could properly aim at them: each went down, in turn, only to stand as if impervious to bullets. He had a horrible feeling that was confirmed as each dropped as if to their hands and knees only to assume the forms of enormous and fiery-eyed wolves. It seemed the rumors were all too accurate. Which meant their guns were no good…

"Here!" he shouted, tossing a knife with a silvered blade to Arlene. There was the tooth of a saint in the hilt and it had been thrice-blessed by an Archimandrite, and it had served him against the Tombstone Vampire.

"Thanks!" The wolves were almost upon them and she held the blade confidently, ready to sell her life dearly.

Leveling his left arm at the nearest wolf, he flexed it so as to discharge a shot from the barrel in the wrist. Although the shot would do no lasting damage to a werewolf, the force of it was enough to bowl it over and buy him a few seconds. He clenched his fist and cocked his elbow to eject the spent shell and load a fresh one, then fired again, blasting one of Arlene's to give her a few seconds grace, before repeating the movement and blasting his second.

Arlene plunged the blessed and silvered blade into the first wolf with practiced ease, killing with a surprising lack of effort. Then, the second was on her.

A wolf slammed into Archer, bowling him over

and he found himself wrestling with it. Lacking an effective weapon, he shoved his left hand into the wolf's mouth as if emulating Tyr and fired. Even if perfectly mundane shot couldn't actually kill it, the mass of lead could certainly blow a large and painful hole in the back of its head and send it spiraling off of him; hopefully it would be out of the fight for a while.

Then, the second wolf was lunging at him. The devil in his chest had gone from purring with pleasure at the opening salvo to seemingly howling with delight as he got to grips with the monsters. Reluctantly, Archer knew he'd have to call upon it for aid: he opened his mouth as the wolf's jaws snapped towards his head and felt the devil surging up and out towards it. A moment later, the wolf was dead. He glanced over at the other one, and saw Arlene tugging the knife from its side, having delivered a killing blow whilst it was stunned, her two already dispatched. She certainly knew how to fight.

Wiping the blade clean on the wolf's fur, she paused to catch her breath for a moment, before returning it to him, saying, "As I said, we might want to watch out for werewolves…"

"Indeed," he replied, drily, sheathing the knife. "I wish it'd been possible to capture one—I would like to know whether this attack was a coincidence or whether Legend and Shootist arranged it somehow."

"Does it really matter?"

"I suppose not," he admitted. "The result's the same, either way. Still, they might have been able to tell us where he was headed."

"Don't worry about that, Marshal, I know."

And, apparently, she did, for she continued to lead him through the forest without a hint of doubt.

"That's our destination," she said, as they left the forest and took a mountain trail; she was pointing at a column of smoke rising from amongst the mountains. It was good to be back out in the sunlight.

"What is it?"

"Have you ever heard of Janson's Folly?"

"The mining town where the Arizona Kid butchered all those people three, four years ago?"

She nodded. "Well, that's where we are headed. After the killing, the miners abandoned the place and bandits began to move in. I heard the dastard asking directions, and it was the direction he headed in."

"I guess it would be an apt place for him to hide out."

"Like flies around the latrine."

"So, I can't talk you out of joining in on this."

She shook her head. "No! No way! I intend to be in on the kill."

"Oh, well… Check your guns and let's head up there. I have a suspicion they may see us coming before we get there, so sneaking in is probably not an option. We just have to make sure we don't provide too easy a target for any sharpshooters who might be watching the trail."

She nodded and began to check her weapons. He checked his arm; wound it up again. They rode on a little way, then dismounted and proceeded on foot, leading their horses. The trail ascended through a steep-sided gulley and, whilst they weren't too exposed, he didn't like feeling so enclosed; he felt vulnerable.

But, there was no ambush, no sniping, nothing. Archer wasn't sure whether to be relieved or worried at what reception they might receive upon entering Janson's Folly. He had his revolver ready in his hand, just in case.

"Keep your eyes peeled," he told her and Arlene used the barrel of her rifle to tap a salute to him.

They arrived at the town—well, it was really little more than a huddle of a dozen buildings in a hollow in the mountainside; dilapidated, poorly-constructed buildings that barely rated being called a settlement at all.

Arlene gave a little shriek and he turned his head to look. A body beneath a pall of flies. He looked more carefully at the silent town, spotted another further away and a third dangling over the rail of a balcony.

"Well, it looks as if Legend and Shootist didn't come to town for a quiet vacation. It seems he was out for revenge or just doesn't like to share. Either that or there was a falling out over something."

"The question," she replied, "is: did he stay or did he move on after killing everyone?"

"Well, we didn't meet him coming down the trail, so, unless we were very unlucky, he must still be here. Even he has to rest sometime!"

They tied their horses loosely to a hitching post and advanced cautiously, guns ready.

Suddenly, a figure stepped out of the shadows, a tall, thin man in a long black duster and wide-brimmed black hat. Legend and Shootist. One of him, anyway; a second appeared in the doorway of a nearby building.

"Archer, hello! Good to see you looking so … well, metallic. Come to finish things, eh? Excellent—I have a bullet with your name on it!" The varmint's voice was unpleasantly affable, as if they were old friends. "And, who is this lovely lady with the firearms and the determined look in her eye?"

"My name is Mrs. Hannigan and you killed my husband, the Sheriff of Norrisville."

"Oh, yes, I remember blowing him away. I take it you desire revenge."

"Yes." Her voice was cold.

Without warning, each of the two halves of the outlaw whipped their guns from their holsters and began to fan them. Archer grabbed Arlene and pulled her down behind a water trough. She dropped her rifle and had to pull out her enormous pistol.

Archer was already returning fire as wood splintered around him and water sprayed. Legend—call this half that for convenience—was moving as he fired and even with his targeter, it was difficult to draw a bead on him, so he raised his left arm and began blasting away with his shotgun. The duster shredded and blood clouded from Legend's leg and he stumbled to his knee; Archer raised his revolver and aimed it right at his forehead and put a slug between his eyes. Legend fell backwards, dead, then vanished.

To Archer's left, Arlene raised her Corpsemaker and fired at Shootist, the enormous slug blowing away half his head. The varmint collapsed back into the building leaving only his black boots visible. Then, the boots and the body to which they were attached, vanished.

"Did you get him?" Archer asked.

"Yes. He vanished."

"So did mine…"

"Bravo! Bravo! I've only been killed once before!"

They turned to see Legend and Shootist standing down the street behind them, gun in hand.

"Oh, hell!" gasped Archer. "There are three of you?"

"More than that, in fact," came another voice.

Looking around, they watched as a fourth stepped from a doorway into the street, then another appeared from an alley, then another and another until they could see a further seven iterations, each armed and with a cruel grin on their face.

"Unfortunately, now, you two shall die…"

"Take cover!" Archer ordered Arlene as he stood to distract them from her. He made sure he was moving so he wouldn't be too easy a target. He fired his revolver and sent one of the varmints falling dead from a balcony, then pulled the trigger again only for it to click empty. He fired the shotgun in his arm twice more, killing another, only to find that was empty. He needed to take cover to reload. A bullet clipped his left arm with a ping and a spark and he flinched at the memory of his last fight with Legend and Shootist.

Arlene fired her huge gun as she rolled, punching an enormous hole in a nearby wall. A second shot as she came to her knees took out another of the villains with an awful chest wound. Her final shot before she was out—the Colt Corpsemaker could only chamber four rounds—went wild as she ducked at a close call.

The devil in Archer's chest was howling with pleasure at all the death and he was finding it hard to concentrate as he tried to find somewhere to hide and reload. He managed to cram a couple of shells into his arm and took down another Legend—there were only four or five left—before the gun jammed. Then, a moment later, a bullet smashed into his thigh and he slumped against a wall.

Legend loomed over Arlene, laughing, leveling his revolver at her. She reached under her skirt and pulled her stiletto out and plunged it into his heart. An expression of pained surprise crossed his features before he vanished from existence.

Archer threw his knife at another of the Shootists, but whilst it embedded deep in the villain's shoulder, he didn't go down. There was nothing else to do; he could hardly think for the howling of the demon.

"Do it," he whispered, then shouted: "Do it!"

He opened his mouth and tendrils of darkness flowed out from inside of him, sweeping towards the remaining Shootists, wrapping around them, crushing, and pushing their way in through noses, mouths, ears and eyes to suffocate and tear at vital elements, killing quickly and painfully.

First one of the figures vanished, leaving twitching darkness behind, then another, leaving just a single one smothered in darkness that retreated to leave him crumpled and broken, lifeless, upon the bloodied ground, as the darkness flowed back into Archer.

He collapsed to the ground and clamped his mouth tightly shut, just in case.

"What the hell was that?" Arlene gasped.

"Exactly! Sorry, I forgot to mention that I have a devil inside of me." He gave a lopsided grin. "I like to keep it inside as it's a devil to control when out."

She shrugged, uncertainly, then pointed at the mangled corpse. "Is he dead?" He understood what she meant.

"Yes, I think so. That body didn't vanish because it must have been his last—the real Legend and

Shootist, if anything was."

"Good." She spat on the body. "Thank you for killing him."

"Thanks for the help. Every part of him that died was a step closer to his final destruction."

He almost couldn't believe it was over, that justice had been served and each of them avenged. He whispered a 'thank you' to the devil in his chest and could sense it was satisfied with the day's work.

The Lights in the Sky are Them/Us

"He was wholly bewildered as to the relation betwixt dream and reality in all his experiences."
— H.P. Lovecraft

Rev. Preacher can't decide
whether those creatures
down in the Old Woods
are devils or angels.
Lots of folks have come upon
their castoffs and droppings
over the years
but no one has actually
seen one or taken a picture.
Oh, forget those fakes
you see in the tabloids—
if you don't know they're a joke
I'll sell you a bridge to heaven.
(Don't tell Rev. Preacher
I said that, by the way.)

Anyway, Ole Doc Flatton
is one of those who believe
They are devils or demons
and he'll point out
all the places in the Old Woods
where fire has scorched
the rocks and clay
in certain secluded groves
and in caves most of us
won't even enter.
Ole Doc can recall
a long list of times
that chants and signing
have been heard in those environs,
even though no one from the town
can explain them.
Passages from scripture
and old books best left alone
are quoted by Ole Doc
to support his demon theory
but most of us can't quite follow.
(He does have followers,
I hasten to add.)

Now, Ma Pendleton
sees it differently.
She's a spiritualist
and talks not of creatures
but of ghosts down there,

or up there—she's not sure which.
When asked how souls of ancestors
could leave evidence
in the Old Woods—
marks on trees, piles of stones,
creeks diverted
from their natural contours—
she smiles her smile
and sings her tune
and that's enough for some.
(She seems a ghost herself
much of the time.)

The high school chemistry
teacher and coach, Mr. Daniels,
is mostly interested in
what little physical evidence
has accumulated—
some tufts of hair
snagged on tree branches,
footprints in photos,
and in plaster casts,
some oddly shaped rocks
neither natural nor aboriginal,
a strange metal object
that appears to be a tool
but for what purpose
no one can say.
Mr. Daniels denies he has a theory
or is writing a book
but when he's had a few
he rambles on
about other dimensions.
(What measurements he has in mind
he'll never say.)

We don't have a Town Drunk
but our next best thing
is Charlie Olander
who was once the sheriff,
now retired,
with lots of time on his hands.
Charlie stays up late,
sometimes all night,
watching the stars
move across the sky
and thinking about the Old Woods
and who might live there.
Well, Charlie lives there,
now that Clara is gone—
he moved into a run-down cabin

by Spring Creek
and has his still going year around
as a hobby and for petty cash.
He talks about the creatures
he's seen out there
and about their flying craft
he thinks come from another galaxy
but won't say why.
(He thinks their X-ray eyes
are what has fried his brain!)

This week Rev. Preacher's sermon
pictured those creatures
down in the Old Woods
as angels come down to save souls
and lead us out of sin.
Last week they were demons from hell
out to lead us into sin
and damn our eternal souls.
All his sermons are popular
so it don't much matter
which way he flip-flops—
he puts on quite a show.
(Don't tell him I said that.)

As for me, I just have
this feeling of Home
but whether those creatures
in the Old Woods
are here to take us home
or are bent on making their home here
I'm just not sure.
(I'm not sure I really want to know…)

— Neal Wilgus

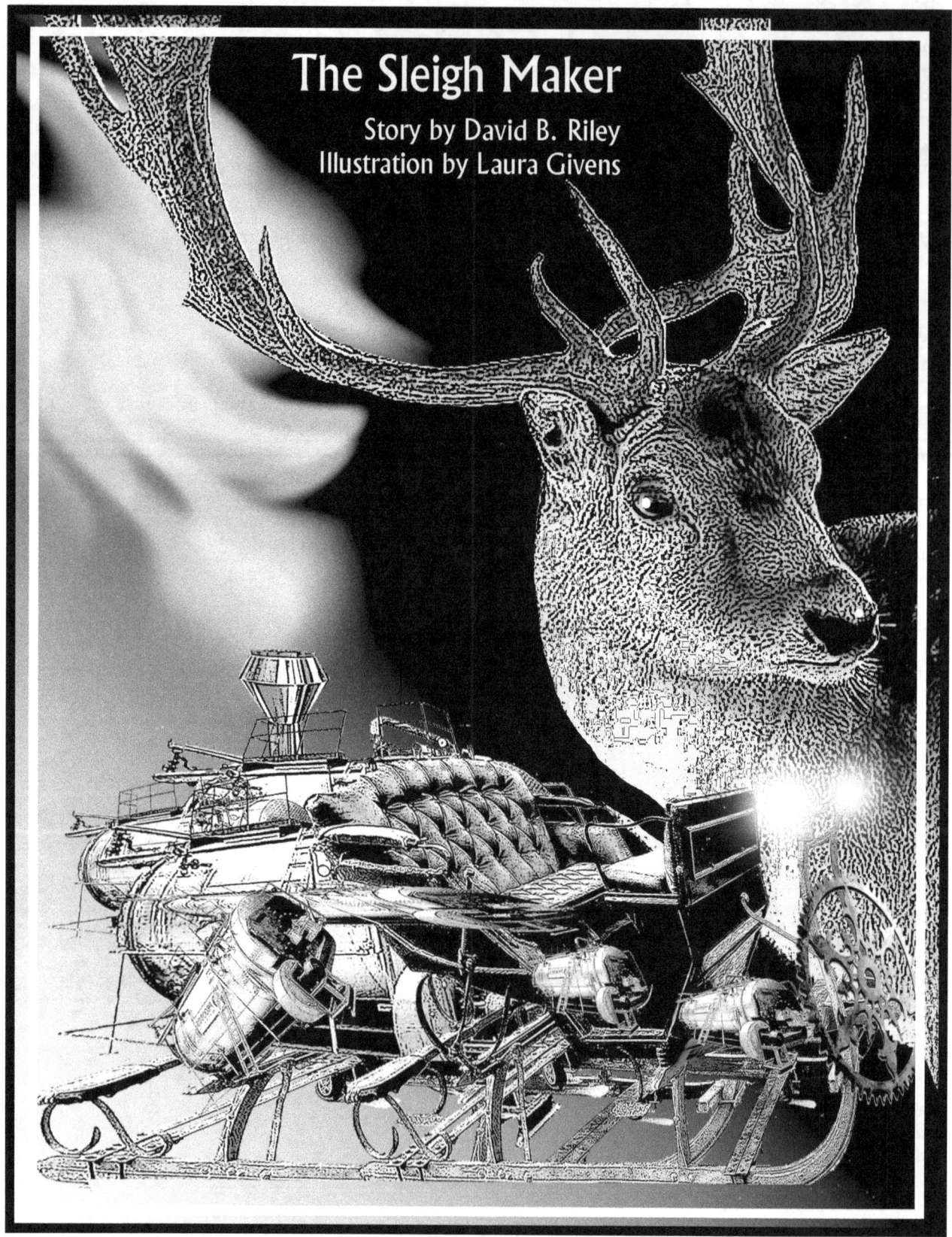

The Sleigh Maker

Story by David B. Riley
Illustration by Laura Givens

Simon turned off the acetylene welder and removed his goggles. That was the last weld. It was done. A year's worth of work finally done. Except for the paint, of course. He'd do that tomorrow. He caught some motion out of the corner of his eye. That damned Blitzen was looking in the window again. Simon shook his fist. "Go on, get out of here!"

He turned out the lights and made sure the heavy gauge steel door was locked, then he headed home for the night. As the Chief Engineer, he had a private cottage all to himself. It was a considerable improvement over the barracks of the toy makers just down the street.

But his accommodations did not matter. It was all about tomorrow. For tomorrow, everyone would be talking about Simon Thomas Tinker. And they would be talking about him for a very long time. Traditional red or a nice shade of blue? He drifted off to sleep dreaming about paint, colorful wonderful paint.

* * *

The boss was munching on a piece of gingerbread as he looked over a letter from a Thea Wilson of San Francisco, California. Young Miss Wilson was extolling on her virtuous behavior during the previous year. And the fact she wanted some model of the submersible ship, *Nautilus*, envisioned by Mister Jules Verne, which she claimed could be obtained from the Emporium store in San Francisco for an astronomical price. And, it apparently had working hatches and such. This seemed an odd gift request for a young girl. He took a sip of coffee. "Give her a rag doll," he declared.

"Uh, I don't think she likes dolls," Elf Randy replied.

"All girls like dolls," the boss insisted.

"Not this one," Elf Randy insisted.

"Put her down for those scary ones with the potato looking heads that give children nightmares. That'll show to ask for a doll if she doesn't like them," the chief decided.

"But she didn't ask for one," Elf Randy pointed out. "The first sentence of her letter specifically says she'd rather have nothing, if she can't get her submarine."

"Then, nothing is what she will have. Next letter," the boss said. "Write it down."

"But isn't that a bit mean? So she wants a submarine? Where's the harm?" Elf Randy asked.

"It's either nothing, or that doll with the creepy eyes. Which is it going to be?"

Elf Randy wrote down "nothing" on the master list. "Next is Billy Swanson, a candidate for a lump of coal if I ever saw one."

"Sir," Elf William was saying. "Sir, it's time for your appointment with the Chief Engineer."

"Oh damn. I'd nearly forgotten." He thought for a moment. "Let's get it over with, then."

* * *

Elliott topped off the water tank, then gently pulled the throttle. The sleigh glided down the street and came to a stop in front of the big house. He set it on idle. The sleigh let out a gasp of steam and then quieted to a gentle purr.

"Why is it blue?" Elf Randy asked. "Sleighs are red."

"That's so passé," Simon said.

"A blue sleigh?" the boss sort of muttered. "I don't know."

"Well, we can paint it any color you want," Simon pointed out. "It's not a problem."

The boss walked around the odd looking sleigh that had no place for reindeer, or any animals to draw it. Instead, there was a purring steam engine. "I don't know."

"It's fast, really fast," Simon said.

The boss stared at it for a moment. "Well, steam, that means stoking coal, does it not?"

"No, nothing of the sort," Simon insisted. "It's using a liquid fuel. Much more efficient—and cleaner, too."

"You know how I feel about whale oil," the boss said.

"No, this is powered by kerosene—the fuel of the future. It'll heat the boiler and the steam will push compressed air through these thrust jets." Simon pointed at his fabulous thrust jets, then reached in and turned the toggle. The jets moved around. It can go up or down or even backwards. "And, no more cold nights. It generates heat. Just pull this lever and you'll be warm. And there's a bonnet you can pull up to keep snow and rain off of you as well. You'll be far more comfortable."

"It's just, we've used reindeer for so long," the boss said.

"And, you remember the cost savings we talked about. This doesn't need expensive hay and oats all year long. It just uses fuel only when you need it," Simon said.

"Well, the reindeer aren't getting any younger," the boss admitted. "But what will become of them?"

Simon opened the side door of his prized invention. "You do remember the barbecue grill I made for you last year?"

"Mmm," Elf Randy said as he patted his tummy and nodded his approval.

"Perhaps a test ride?" Simon asked. "See what it can do?"

"Well, I guess that would be prudent, to check it out and all," the boss agreed.

"You're not getting in that thing!" a woman was suddenly yelling.

"Mrs. C.," Simon said. He'd been hoping to avoid this moment. He'd actually scheduled this demonstration when she usually took her nap. Mrs. C. and Simon had a history—a bad history. She hated every single one of his ideas. She even hated the barbecue grill, because it made so much smoke.

"We were just going to try it out," Simon explained.

"I don't think something like that could possibly be safe. And, besides, we don't need it. We've gotten by just fine for years," she said. "Come inside, it's cold out here."

So, they all went inside. Simon explained how he'd built the sleigh and taken every precaution. Mrs. C remained unconvinced. Finally, he offered a suggestion. "This is the future," Simon said. "Tell you what, just sit out there on the porch, both of you, and I'll take it up and give you a demonstration to show you some of the things it can do."

"Well, dearest, I guess we owe him that much," the boss agreed.

"Okay, but why is it blue? Sleighs are supposed to be red?" Mrs. C asked. "I know we have plenty of red paint."

They all went back outside. The boss and Mrs. C took up their favorite rocking chairs on the porch and Simon climbed in and switched the steam engine to run. He turned the thruster to up and pulled on the throttle. The sleigh lifted up and took off into the sky. In seconds it looked as if he was even going to be able to reach out and touch the aurora borealis itself. He turned up the brightness of the side lanterns so they'd be able to see him down in the village. He banked the sleigh into an arch, then tried a corkscrew pattern. Surely that would impress them.

Then the sleigh started to rock. The steam thrusters were acting up. He looked at the glowing radium painted dials and saw the steam pressure was plummeting. That wasn't right. The sleigh could run for hours. And then he noticed another gauge that was even more alarming. The temperature was sky high on the boiler.

He looked at the manifold. It was actually glowing. That couldn't possibly be happening. He'd only been up for a few minutes. It was as if there was no water in the boiler. But he'd just filled it up. He started looking for a quick place to put it down as he cut power. Another fear, a design flaw he'd only just then thought off, occurred to him. With the manifold that hot, not only could the boiler explode as the steel weakened from the heat, just as train engines often did, but the kerosene fuel line was getting dangerously hot as well.

Some motion caught his eye on the right. It was that damned Blitzen. The blasted reindeer was flying alongside the sleigh. "You!" It suddenly all made sense. The reindeer must've drained the water from the boiler when they were inside. He shook his fist at Blitzen and suddenly wished he'd taken the reindeer's snooping around more seriously.

Blitzen responded by sticking his tongue out at him, then turning and flying away. A few seconds later, Simon's curiosity about which one would go first was answered. It was the fuel. The sleigh exploded into a ball of fire that could easily be seen from the village below.

"Looks like you were right, mother," the boss said.

"Seems the damned fool blew himself up. Let's go inside. It's cold out here," Mrs. C. suggested.

They would definitely be talking about Simon Tinker for a very long time.

tail in Winnipeg
ice dragon raises blind eyes
in Wisconsin

— Sandra Lindow

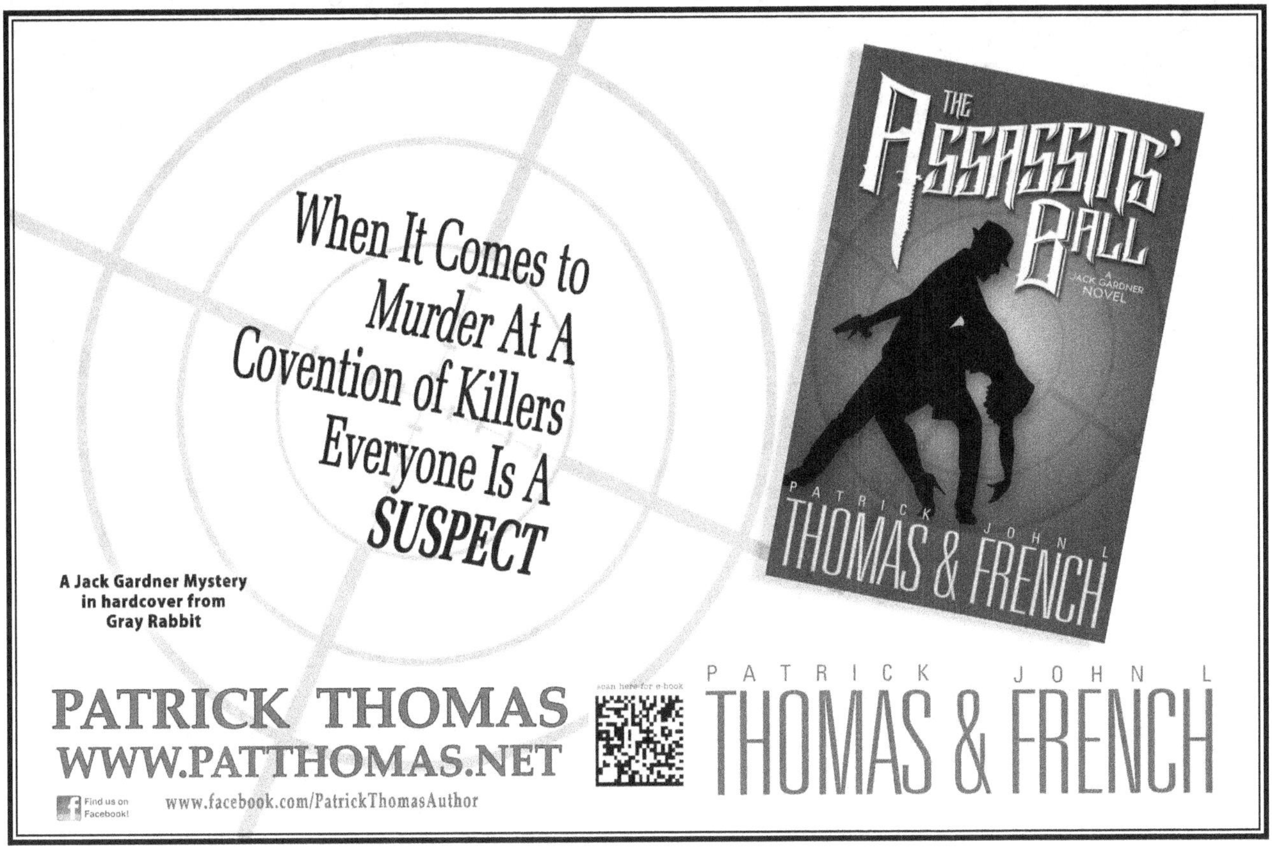
When It Comes to
Murder At A
Covention of Killers
Everyone Is A
SUSPECT
THE ASSASSINS' BALL
A JACK GARDNER NOVEL
PATRICK JOHN L
THOMAS & FRENCH
A Jack Gardner Mystery
in hardcover from
Gray Rabbit
PATRICK THOMAS
WWW.PATTHOMAS.NET
scan here for e-book
Find us on Facebook!
www.facebook.com/PatrickThomasAuthor
PATRICK JOHN L
THOMAS & FRENCH

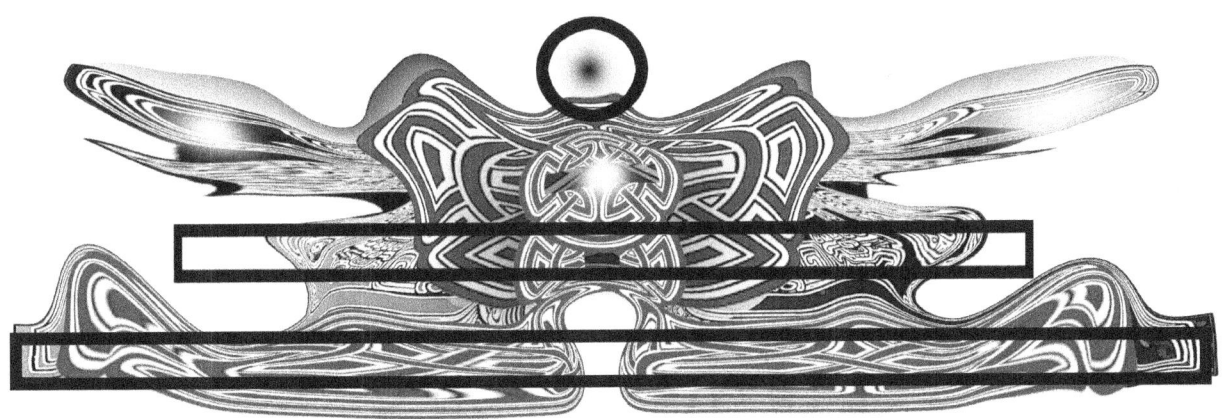

The Spellweaver & the Once Proud Prince

Story by
Jim Lee

Illustration by
Erika McGinnis

Many centuries ago in a far and obscure corner of an equally distant and little known kingdom, there lived a young Spellweaver named Lema. She was, like most of us, neither astoundingly beautiful nor particularly ugly. But she was strong and healthy, and well-schooled in the several Great Magicks.

She endeavored to use her skills wisely, for the betterment of all who could pay—and sometimes, if she was of a mind, for those who could not.

No, Lema was no saint. Nor was she an ambitious monster. She was simply a woman of skill, intelligence and decent ethics. In due course, she found herself in love with a fine and daring young man.

He was a Patriot, in the best of all senses—honest, capable and fair-minded. Unfortunately such virtues made him seem strange to some—perhaps even dangerous.

And so it was that the Patriot was branded an Outlaw.

The local Prince ordered his soldiers into the woodlands to hunt the young man down. This Prince was a tall man, going prematurely gray and had once been both proud and brave.

But ten years earlier, Good King Tarn had died without leaving a clear successor. Accordingly, the Great Council of the Several Principalities met to elect a new King. They passed over the local Prince (most unfairly, he thought) in favor of his slightly older cousin.

To his credit, the Prince was not the sort to rebel against lawful authority. Yet he dwelled over-long on this perceived injustice. He grew ever-more bitter, year by year as a sick, unfocused anger rose up inside him. His pride took on a destructive character and he eventually became an outright Tyrant—taking out his frustrations on the people.

The King, his cousin, sat with apparent indifference in the distant Capital City of the Kingdom. He might not have fully approved of the local Prince's methods, but had no taste for intervening as long as his personal authority was not threatened.

So it was that many good men and women found it necessary to plot against the Prince. The Patriot was, as you might have guessed, among them. Soon the land was torn by a sputtering, small scale but violent Civil War.

However, no one knew of the Patriot and the Spellweaver's secret romance. They met quietly and often in the virgin forests beyond Lema's small cottage. There they did the things that lovers will—holding hands and strolling about together, gazing at one another for long moments in eloquent silence and then speaking in sweet whispered tones of things both great and unimportant.

The Spellweaver also used her powers to keep her lover safe, as one would expect in such circumstances. Her subtle efforts and the Patriot's martial skills frustrated the Prince for many months. But in the autumn of that year, just prior to harvest time, the Patriot was betrayed.

Before any knew the better, the Prince had him captured and tortured for information. Learning nothing of value, the enraged Prince ordered the young man tied and thrust helpless into an icy mountain lake until drowned. Then the Patriot was quickly buried in a shallow, unmarked grave—so that the resistance could not claim him as a martyr.

In time the Patriot's fate came to be known and the young Spellweaver was heartbroken. She turned her arcane abilities to locating her love's grave.

Once there, she threw herself down and rolled in the dirt like a madwoman. But then she rose, straightened her soiled clothing and went off, to prepare her vengeance.

Three days later, the still-loose ground began to stir.

It took till long after nightfall, but the Spellweaver was in no great hurry. She stood by patiently, watched as her lover's corpse slowly freed itself from its unconsecrated resting spot. It was the most difficult and dangerous Magick that Lema had ever worked and in one sense it was all in vain, of course. She might well reanimate the Patriot's stinking corpse, but the essences of the man she loved—his heart and soul, his spirit and mind—were all gone forever.

Yes, even the Great Magicks have their limits—as she well knew.

Nonetheless, the Spellweaver gave the lifeless thing its instructions in a compulsively self-controlled monotone. Then she watched it shamble carelessly from sight.

Only after it disappeared from her view did she allow herself to weep.

The Patriot's corpse reached the principality's major town near midday. It advanced unchallenged to the Prince's Citadel. There the first of several guards found the courage to attempt to block the dead thing's path. This stout warrior was flung aside, as was the next and the next and the next.

In total, a dozen well-armed men were met and defeated by the uncaring invader. Not even one was killed, however. Lema had been very precise in her instructions: Mere common soldiers, sworn to follow their better's orders, were to be disarmed or disabled, rendered unconscious should the need arise—but none of these were to be slain.

In any case, what harm such men could do their grotesque opponent was negligible. The Patriot was already dead. His moldering corpse knew no sensation, felt no pain.

At last, the walking dead thing found the wide-eyed Prince—no longer proud or brave—cowering behind his throne. It took hold of him by the scruff of the neck. Up a winding staircase they went, the corpse's arm extended full-length in front of him, his gurgling captive unwittingly in the lead.

They emerged near the top of the Citadel's primary tower, on a balcony that overlooked the open courtyard where the town's population was often required to gather, to hear the Prince give his ever-more bombastic speeches and ill-tempered proclamations.

The corpse did not hesitate or pause, nor did it make haste. It simply advanced, steadily and remorseless, to the very edge of the outer railing. Its right arm now rigidly extended into empty space, its hand still clutched the gasping Prince by his expensive collar.

"Somebody help me!" the Prince moaned, dangling in mid-air.

Down in the courtyard, an archer took aim and fired. The shaft lodged near the shoulder of the corpse, but the thing's arm never so much as wavered.

And even through his panic, the Prince realized that it was a good thing—as he was suspended a great distance above his potential landing place. The fearful man saw this and his eyes bulged even more so than before. He sputtered again, begging the archer not to fire again.

Meanwhile, the Prince's Lieutenant and two swordsmen came bounding up the stairs. They paused a few arm's-lengths behind the animated dead man, indecisive.

The Lieutenant called down, ordered the bowman away. Then he turned and watched something as thick and cold and sticky as the region's fabled maple syrup oozed from the corpse's arrow-damaged upper arm. A trail of it seemed to briefly defy gravity, moving as it did sideways to the dead man's wrist before slowly dribbling down its quivering prisoner's neck.

Whatever the pus-colored substance was, it most surely wasn't blood!

The Lieutenant glanced at the swordsman who stood adjacent to his muscular shoulder and shook his head in bewilderment. What do I do now?

"You stay a safe distance away," a female voice answered his unspoken question.

The Lieutenant and his men turned.

They recognized the young Spellweaver from the far dell—the one who was always curing sick goats and casting Spells of Protection for the region's children.

"And now," she continued, "you shall listen to my demands."

The small, unarmed woman took a step forward. Behind her, more soldiers waited on the stairs. One stepped forward, his dagger raised—but the Lieutenant shook his head.

"You caused this? You control this ... ah, creature?"

"He had a name!" she cried out.

"Of course." The Lieutenant nodded. "But it no longer matters, does it?"

"Perhaps not. But if you wish your Prince to survive ...?"

This time the Lieutenant shrugged. "I am sworn to serve him."

"Well, I summoned his captor from the very earth. Only I can return him to his rest, or give the order that will safely free your liege."

"And should we be unable to comply with your demands?"

The answer was obvious to all, even the panic-stricken Prince.

"No!" he shrilled. "Do anything! Do whatever she wants! Quickly, quickly!"

The Spellweaver looked the Lieutenant in the eye. "A brave fellow, isn't he? But in any case, my demands. First, you will make no attempt to challenge or interfere with my ... agent. Agreed? He shall hold your Prince as he is now, for the next ten days and nights."

"Like that?" The Lieutenant arched a thick brow. "Out in the weather? No food or drink? He'll die."

"If you interfere, he certainly will. But no, one of your soldiers, unarmed, shall be permitted near enough to leave food and water from time to time. It shall be placed upon the railing, within reach of my ... agent's free hand. Our Good Prince shall have his food and drink passed to him, from the hand of one he had murdered. And the food shall consist of the gruel prisoners of his dungeon receive; the drink—water only, absolutely no wine or milk or juice. And that shall be the tepid, impure well water from the peasant's emergency reserve. As to the weather, be assured: I have woven a Spell of Limited Protection around him. He shall not freeze, though on the third, fourth and eighth nights he is likely to be rained on quite a bit!"

"What of his … bodily functions?"

"He must relieve himself there. I expect the lower quarter of his Royal finery shall be quite ruined and he will begin to smell bad shortly. But with my agent in such close proximity, I doubt many will notice by comparison."

The Lieutenant frowned then nodded.

"Additionally, the town folk are to be allowed—no, encouraged!—to come and see their Prince in this state. If some choose to jeer or make foul comment, so be it—I require your sacred word that they will not be punished. But attendance shall not be mandatory—none of our Beloved Prince's bully-and-blackguard tactics, Lieutenant."

"Understood. And then?"

"At dawn of the eleventh day, I shall order the Prince brought safely back onto this balcony. I shall then turn myself unresistingly over to your justice, with the single proviso that, when I send my helper back to his grave, he shall receive a proper funeral rite."

The Lieutenant's dark eyes narrowed. "That is all?"

"That is all," Lema confirmed.

And so it was done. And the people came. They stood in silence, that first day. On the second, a few made cautious gestures. By the third day, the braver souls shouted derision. By the fifth, the Once-Proud Prince was being regularly pelted with garbage. Even some of his grim-faced soldiers cracked quick, ugly, semi-secret grins.

The Spellweaver's enemy was hopelessly insane long before the ten days and nights were up. The inherent danger of the situation, and conversely the impossible boredom, the rancid food and water, the building ridicule and constant humiliation—all these played their parts in the Tyrant Prince's complete mental collapse.

By the dawn of the eleventh day, when the Patriot's decaying corpse was told to swing round and deposit its burden on the cool stone of the balcony, the Once-Proud Prince was no more. In his place was a pathetic, haggardly creature who hardly minded eating swill and quite cheerfully fouled its own stinking garments.

Lema, who had forced herself to watch as four disgusted servants picked up their former liege and carried him, at the Lieutenant's order, to the hospital, now sent her 'agent' away.

Then she leaned out across the railing and was quietly sick.

She half-expected a dagger in the back and would not have minded such an outcome over-much.

But what she received was somehow worse.

The Lieutenant placed a strong yet sympathetic hand upon her shoulder.

The Spellweaver turned her head, met his eyes then shrugged.

"You must have hated him greatly—why else put yourself through all of this? He did many things in his time—for good as well as ill, though mostly for ill of late. He could be harsh, often to excess. But … I am curious…?"

"I loved him." Somehow, Lema smiled. "The one I just sent off? When he died—"

"Yes, I understand." The big man's expression was sincere. "But this region is now without a ruler."

"You can surely move up," she said. "I cannot imagine the King would object, you having been a loyal soldier under the Prince. And your first decision: my punishment!"

"I could by all rights kill you," the Lieutenant agreed. "But I believe I know a worse fate—or at least one that seems strangely fitting. You, Spellweaver, have taken our Prince from us. It shall be your burden to replace him!"

She stared at him in disbelief. "The King—his own cousin!"

"I have served both men. The King cares not a whit who runs this sleepy backwater, as long as the taxes are paid, his name is respected and there is something like order. You could bring peace to us, after which all else would follow most naturally."

Lema saw that he was serious—and more, determined that it should be so.

And so it happened: Lema accepted for herself a life of unending burden and responsibility. She tried to govern well, this Spellweaver-turned-Ruler.

For the larger part, she succeeded, which is perhaps all that any could by rights hope for. In the fullness of time, the King did more than tolerate her—he went so far as to formerly recognize her position and grant limited sovereignty to the Principality. She saw that her lands were well-maintained and paid the taxes on time, while keeping her subjects reasonably content—far more so than her predecessor had managed, to say the least!

By the time that advancing age began to stalk

the Spellweaver she had adopted an orphan child with talent. She schooled the child in the complex ways of Power, both Magickal and Mundane—and even more important, in the limits of such things.

Thus began to fabled Dynasty of the Orphans. That long, unbroken chain of Spellweaving Princesses and Princes which some claim continues to this very day, and which just might last forever in that far and obscure corner of that distant and little-known Kingdom.

Spider Woman Stories

Her web glistens in the sunrise sunlight,
Spider Woman spinning silk
between the slender sandstone spires of Spider Rock.
Your children are born as beasts,
capable of nothing more than grunting, eating and pooping.
Until one day as parents you teach your child a word
such as the word for bird
and suddenly this magnificent winged creature,
an airborne acrobat,
is reduced to a label
but once something has a name
it can become a character in one of Spider Woman's stories.
These stories will link names together strand by strand
until Spider Woman has created a glistening web of mythology.
These stories will teach your children how to behave.
These stories will provide seeds for your children's dreams
until their songs will take wing,
then and only then will they become full-fledged human beings.
At sunrise, Spider Woman spins her silken strands
between the slender sandstone spires of Spider Rock
weaving stories and catching dreams.

— Gary Every

Demon Fire

Outside: the harbor,
the town wall, both extant.

Inside: No trace of wood.
No leather. No cloth.
No birds, no insects.
The wells dried out.
The mud burnt brick hard.
A few stone buildings.
Ash. Charred bones.
Two kings (alive),
their guards
at a short distance.

"Too few bones," said Donal,
the Red King: red-haired,
red-handed in war.
"We think most people
were taken prisoner,
or killed elsewhere."

"Several escaped," said Xau,
"and fled to us eight days ago."

"At moon dark," said Donal.
"And last month, the same thing—
a town obliterated at moon dark."

He led Xau to the town center.
The stone fountain bowl
had cracked in two.
On the flagstones in front:
a black circle,
wide as a man's height,
wavy lines radiating from it.

"Demon sign," said Xau.

"Yes." Donal spat on the sign.
"Help us. Name your terms."

"We'll help. No terms," said Xau.
"But how? What can we do?"

"I don't know," said Donal.
"I knew how to fight you.
I have no idea how to fight this."

They stood, silent,
by the dry fountain
at the center of what
had once been a town.

— Mary Soon Lee

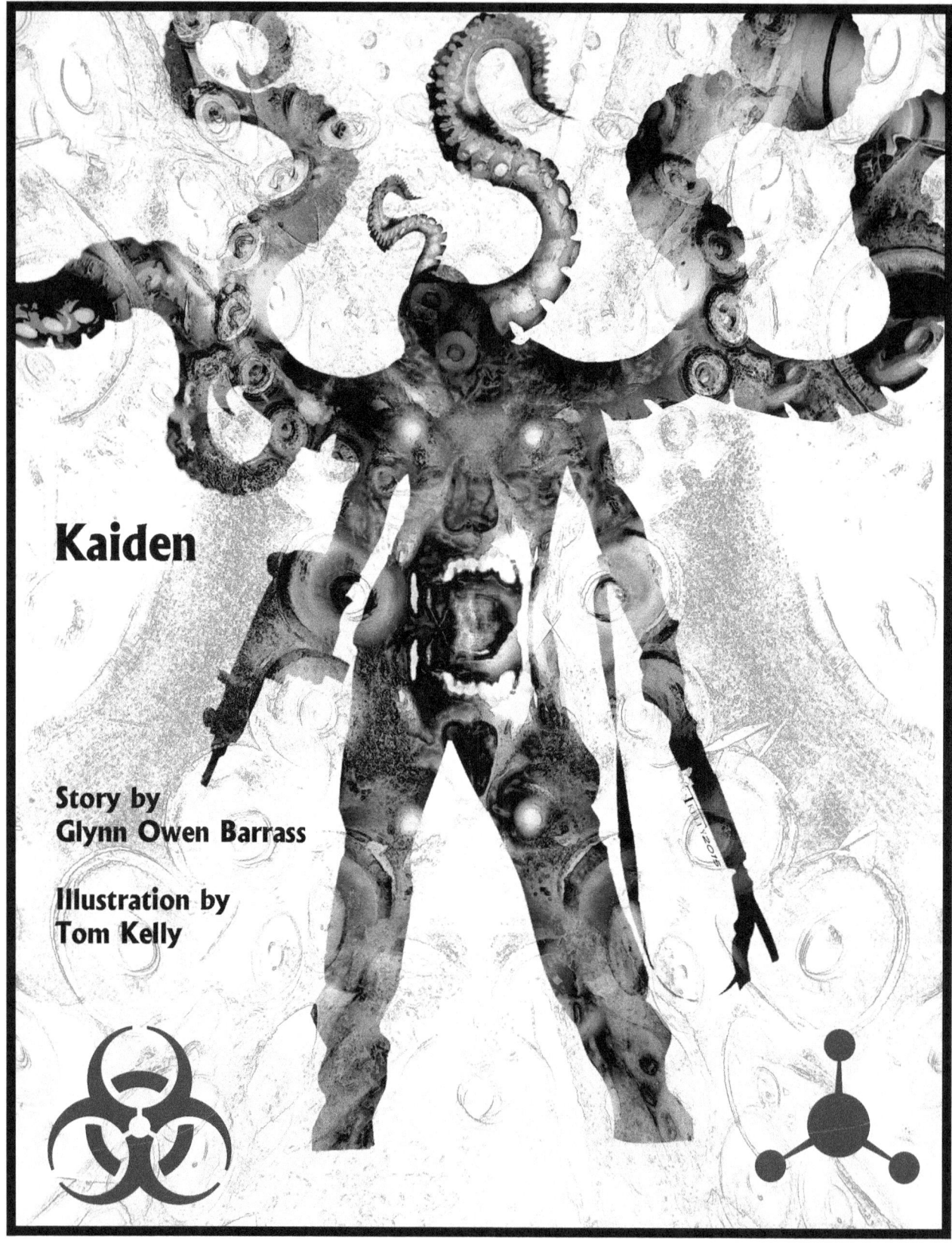

Kaiden

Story by
Glynn Owen Barrass

Illustration by
Tom Kelly

Now

Kaiden, finishing his quick meal of cold roasted rat, rubbed grease-stained hands against his black combat fatigues. Coated in muck already, the action didn't do much except ensure the shotgun he retrieved from the weed-thick cobbles wouldn't slip in his hands. He stood from his crouch, stretched his legs, then examined the shotgun while twisting the kinks from his neck. Double barrelled, chipped metal and scarred wood, he had two shells loaded and a handful in his pockets. The shotgun then went into his handmade leather shoulder holster. Kaiden knelt again, picked up the ripped, greasy foil his meal was wrapped in, and folded it, tucking it into the side pocket of his fatigues.

Thick green bushes on three sides surrounded the place he'd chosen to sit and eat in, the small front yard of a house abandoned for decades, anonymous in a row of identical houses. Behind him stood a sagging front door beside a bay window opaque with dirt. Kaiden turned, licked his finger and approached the window. Using his saliva he drew a large smiley face in the muck, then turned back and approached the bushes.

The front gate leading to the road was overgrown with foliage—he'd been forced to squeeze then fall through to enter the yard. Now he crept and slowly parted the branches to peer out and examine the world beyond. He saw weather-worn pavements, a cracked road overgrown by Mother Nature, and facing him, a row of houses with hemmed in yards like his own.

No sounds of obscenities stalking the asphalt on sharp, chitinous toes. No telltale stink of ammonia and upturned graves. He left the yard only a little warily, checking both ends of the road and the sky for things hunting sanity and flesh. A spattering of clouds, a dull yellow mid-afternoon sun; Kaiden felt safe.

16 Hours Ago

The blowtorch in Kaiden's hand sputtered and fell empty. It was okay though, the things were decimated, well and truly dead. He tossed the blowtorch to the ground and wiped sour tasting soot from his mouth. At his feet lay the remnants of three spider-legged orbs, nicknamed 'wrigglies' by his people, the things that had caused so much trouble over the past few days. They were almost ash now, no longer singing the song of madness and death that had attacked their minds. They lay with the trash, the broken bottles and rotted vegetables. Still they succeeded in looking obscene and alien despite being naught but black lumps. Hearing footsteps behind him, Kaiden turned to see Cassandra, beautiful Cassandra, in dirty orange boiler suit with the legs and sleeves ripped off, her long red hair held up with a bow of old pink knickers.

"Heh," she said, "we've buried Ron and Tizzy."

Kaiden nodded, looked down. Her hands were black with mud.

She followed his eyes and rubbed her hands together, clearing them partially. "Who'd have thought it, huh? The wrigglies did more harm dead than alive."

Kaiden sighed and kicked the blowtorch. "Damned idiot Professor Tollender, bringing them here in the first place." He walked past Cassandra, she following quickly at his side. A few steps later and they were away from the smelly jungle of rubbish the camp called 'The Recycling Centre,' and approaching the rusted corrugated walls of the main compound.

"He went out again you know." Kaiden turned at her words and saw her grimace. "Fucking idiot," she added.

Just as Kaiden reached for the compound's plastic sliding door, the alarm klaxons sounded.

Now

He moved down the road slowly, cautiously, as he would any area he wasn't familiar with. The monsters could appear at any time, and although there were no tell-tale spores or slime trails, he knew they must pass this way because he was so close to their source. He looked to the dark windows and sagging roofs and considered a world before the monsters. Calm and beautiful, he guessed. Cassandra came to mind and he fought back a sob.

Kaiden shook his head. Attached to a yard wall he saw a grubby white sign. He paused, knelt, and rubbed it with the end of his combat jacket wrapped around his fist. 'Crescent Road,' the sign said, and he glanced to the end of said road knowing his destination lay just beyond. He walked on and tried to keep the image of Cassandra from his mind, failing for the most part until he reached the road's termination and saw the scene beyond.

Crescent Road flanked another road, this one similar in decrepitude but opening out to its left onto a large grassy area overgrown with wildflowers. Beyond stood the park, 'Albert Park' the iron letters said above the broken double gates, the park beyond so overgrown the surrounding fences bulged with tree branches, the two walls surrounding the gates thick with lichen and ivy.

The gates, bent outwards and hanging from the walls that bore their hinges, looked to have burst from the inside as if something huge had escaped. As far as Kaiden knew, it probably had.

He froze and crouched as dark shapes came skittering from those gates. Wrigglies, dozens of them, not rushing in his direction but rather past the hulking, ivy-covered building to the park's right. The sight of the things made Kaiden snarl. They had caused so much horror recently, yet they still weren't the worst he could encounter. There was the thing in the park for a start.

16 Hours Ago

Kaiden and Cassandra turned left instead of entering the compound, their footsteps becoming a run as they turned right at the corner then straight on towards the main gate. They approached the compound's tall concrete walls with shared trepidation. This was the second time in two days the alarm had been activated. The source: Dubois on the roof of the gatehouse, a sniper rifle in one hand and the other winding the klaxon. He wore patchwork plate and leather armour, telescoping goggles pulled up on shaved head.

Dubois saw Kaiden, Cassandra, and three more rushing towards him from other directions, and ceased working the alarm. He raised his rifle two-handed, pointing it beyond the gate.

"He's back!" Dubois yelled. "He's back and he's in bad company."

Kaiden rushed towards the steel plate and mesh gate, his feet stumbling to a halt in the dirt beside the gatehouse. Rick the Brick and Captain Swanson were fast beside him, then Cassandra and Little Mo. All stared in silence at the scene beyond the gate.

"Oh shit," Little Mo broke it with her lisping voice.

Around a hundred metres from the gate, growing closer by the second, white-haired Professor Tollender drove the compound's stripped down Humvee erratically down the dirt path. The man was naked except for his goggles, high top trainers and boxer shorts. And, he wasn't alone. Not just the dead things piled up in the back of the Humvee—more wrigglies he'd brought back to experiment on, the creatures whose still animate brains had caused a murder and two suicides in the compound already. A pack of sixty or so living specimens skittered after Tollender. He was around eighty metres from the gate now.

An explosion of gunfire made Kaiden duck involuntarily. All heads looked up to see Dubois reload another round into his rifle. He took aim through the sights. Kaiden turned and watched the approaching convoy.

Sixty-five metres now, and the next shot missed the professor again.

"Shoot the engine, the engine!" Captain Swanson shouted.

Kaiden turned to the man and saw him produce a gun from the folds of his tatty brown trench coat. He had a glint of steely determination in his eyes as he pointed the Glock 17 between the fence wires.

Fifty metres and closing, Kaiden noticed the professor's deranged expression, the blood pouring from his nose past his giggling mouth.

Captain Swanson opened fire, shot after shot piercing the Humvee's engine but not doing a jot to halt its terminal progress. Another shot from Dubois and the professor's head exploded, eliciting a small 'whoop' from the crowd and a short lived smile to Kaiden's lips. The headless corpse slumped forward, the Humvee continued towards the compound.

Forty metres, and the wrigglies awful psychic buzzing appeared in Kaiden's skull.

Captain Swanson's gun clicked empty.

Kaiden felt a hand gripping his own. Cassandra.

Thirty metres.

Twenty.

Now

All gone, everyone dead in an orgy of slaughter that Kaiden had run from like a coward. But what could he have done, really? He'd seen the way the wind was blowing and escaped after witnessing his love Cassandra fall dead from the knife Little Mo shoved into her chest. This was after Dubois had blown his own brains out, the wrigglies storming the gate alongside Tollender's vehicle screaming in Kaiden's head to KILL, KILL, KILL AND KILL YOURSELF!

He'd run, grabbed some provisions and a gun, then started his journey towards the source of all the death and destruction.

The park.

He waited until the wrigglies disappeared from view, crept slowly to the corner, then poked his head around to watch them charge away down the road beyond the park. Kaiden took a deep breath, looked around, and headed towards the park himself. Without much cover to go with, he ran in a crouch, from one bush or patch of flowers to another.

Overgrown from a distance, close up the thick trees intimidated with their shadows, their reaching, clutching branches. Still, it was a far safer bet than stepping through the open gate the wrigglies had just passed through.

He paused near the fence and examined the building to his right. The words above the smashed glass doors had many letters missing and he read: 'D__mans Muse__.' *Museum maybe?* His eyes dropped to something fronting the building that although thick with weeds resembled ... *a cannon? I wonder if it still works?* Then other thoughts appeared such as: *did the building hold more weapons, clothing?* He chose to leave such speculations for later explorations, should there be a later.

He made a final sprint to the gates, found a spot to squeeze through, and poked his shotgun forwards to help lever himself through the foliage. It was a tough squeeze, the branches attacking him as he got further in, but spitting out leaves and rubbing cobwebs from his face, Kaiden made it through to the park proper.

The scene before him was heavily overgrown, once cultivated trees, flowers and bushes making the park resemble a huge wilderness. It smelled glorious.

Old paths were virtually invisible except for a few stones apparent between the grass and weeds, the visibility poor beyond the nearby trees. Kaiden knew which direction to go however, and stepping across high grass, thick with crunching leaves and the shells of flowers gone to seed, he walked with determination towards the park's centre. There were no signs of monsters, but also no birds, bees or other insects. At the forest of trees he paused, for there was something ... off about them. Yes, the branches resembled human limbs, the trunks similar to human chests and the boles certainly resembling human faces. Using the shotgun, Kaiden poked the nearest tree and found its surface rubbery, not like bark at all. Then, one of the faces wailed.

Kaiden stumbled back, fell right on his backside, but composed himself quickly and got back on his feet. The tree made no more noise, the forest didn't move to attack him, and with nowhere to go but forward, he braced himself and entered.

The smell within the forest was far from glorious, for he soon detected an organic smell hinting of sweat and faeces. It was too dark inside; the noises around him, noises he'd rather were the gentle rustle of leaves, sounded more like whispers to Kaiden's nervous imagination. Had the trees once been people? What happened in the park when reality broke and the horrors fell from the sky? Before his time, thankfully. He passed the final trees mentally unprepared for what stood beyond, and froze, chills filling his body.

I've seen this before, but it hasn't gotten any easier.

Past the mutated trees, down a short hilly rise, stood his destination, a huge ellipsoid dug into the earth surrounded by a bent iron fence. 'No Fishing,' ordered the one remaining sign above the fence, but there was no water regardless.

One of the *things* had made its home here, death and madness replacing the lake with bubbling grey flesh and thick white tendons that bridged the viscous muck that formed its unclean flesh. Located roughly near the centre, a bulbous shape the size of a house protruded from the mass. A head of sorts, it bore a gigantic face that tried to look human but failed miserably. The warped eyelids were closed. He guessed it was asleep.

Kaiden approached and the smell, hitting him in a wall of foulness, made him gag—the stink of decay and rotten fruit a thousand times over making him cover his mouth as he squeezed between the bars.

He paused within, looked for the largest, safest tendon to step upon, finding one a few metres to his right. After taking a deep breath from behind his hand he removed the shotgun from its holster and stepped upon alien flesh. The tendon vibrated, giving Kaiden the impression of being a fly in a web, but the spider at its centre did not move from its slumber.

Kaiden tried walking with confidence, to think confidently. He was beginning to succeed when, as he neared the end of the tendon, a painful buzzing filled his head, turning him weak at the knees and making him stumble. Kaiden looked down past the tendon and saw, within the shifting filth, the small, embryonic forms of wrigglies cocooned in transparent shells. There were hundreds of them, all different sizes. One of the larger specimens must have noticed him in its slumber, he guessed. The buzzing did not return.

Kaiden gripped his shotgun tighter and stepped onto another tendon at an angle to his, twisting down into the flesh before him. He was a third of the way to the being and was already sweating considerably.

"Don't back out now," he whispered, and carefully approached while hopping from tendon to tendon. Soon the 'head' shadowed him, and Kaiden knew there was no turning back.

A huge white hump, it had hundreds of thin red veins visible beneath its skin and in some places, the mere hints of movements from pumping, purple organs or muscles. Eyes, lidded eyes larger than Kaiden's whole body, stood roughly where they would be on a human head, but these were stretched and warped into smaller eyes winding round the bulk. A drooping nose above a twisted slit of a mouth gave the obscene being the resemblance of something formed from wax left too long in the sunlight or an aborted monstrosity spat from a diseased womb.

Kaiden stared while pointing his shotgun in nervous hands. There was no movement except for the bubbling pits around him, then, the gigantic eyelid to his left flickered, the eye pulsing beneath. He took a step back as it opened partially, the bottom of the lid spilling rivulets of yellow pus as a dark brown eyeball appeared with a hint of blood red iris. The mouth parted, revealing a breathing darkness with a stench so powerful it almost made Kaiden vomit on the spot. He choked a little, and spoke.

"It's me, me again. You remember don't you? When I tried killing you and we made the deal?" Many months ago, when things worse than wrigglies had killed his people, Kaiden had gone monster hunting, turned up at the lake with a Humvee filled with petrol cans, and this being, this *deity*, had spoken to him.

The eyelid opened further, the blood red eye turning slowly, the pupil a black horizontal slit reflecting Kaiden's pleading face.

"You can bring them back again, yes? Or at least the woman, Cassandra?"

Something like a low chuckle issued from the being's mouth.

Kaiden went to his knees. "Please, do this again. What's a world without humans? What would you monsters do without us?"

The giant eye widened, the pupil expanding to fill the iris with black. Kaiden saw himself in that reflection and more—he saw something behind him, some hulking, squirming form.

He shuffled round and held back a scream. The form had appeared in silence, a thing roughly resembling a giant eight-fingered hand. Formed from grey, ulcerous flesh, the bulbous fingers were crisscrossed with thick blue veins. Kaiden dropped his shotgun and scurried backwards as one of the fingers split vertically, froze at what was revealed inside.

Cassandra?

Almost Cassandra, her naked form smothered in a greenish-yellow paste. Blue organic tubes filled her mouth, nostrils and private parts, pumping methodically as her body shivered. The tubes were connected to the grey tissue inside the shell, linking Cassandra's clone to the being's appendage.

After a few moments of shock and revulsion, the reality of the situation hit Kaiden. *It agreed! Thank you!*

Another finger split, this one revealing Professor Tollender's naked form. *We could do without him, I think*, Kaiden thought. Then came Rick the Brick and Little Mo. The next finger, Kaiden was expecting another friend from the compound. It shuddered, split from top to bottom like a peapod, and revealed … himself.

"What the?" Kaiden gasped, shook his head at the sight of his duplicated form twitching there like the others. He stood, turned, and his horror grew at the being's huge curved grin, all eyes open and staring straight at him.

The being issued a low grumble, a fetid, stinking thunder, and Kaiden, through his shock, realized that he was hearing a laugh.

"No more deals huh," he said with a bravado he didn't feel. He kneeled slowly with the intention of retrieving his dropped shotgun. He didn't get far.

NO MORE DEALS, a deep voice tore through his skull. Pale shapes flopped from the being's mouth, like slimy albino eels but longer, pulsing with hideous motion. The mouth opened wider, and the tongues rolled in a torrent towards Kaiden's prone, defenceless body.

As Kaiden was engulfed, a strange revelation came to him: "this isn't the first time I've died." His following scream was terminated as the tongues sucked him into the mouth. A moment later, all that remained of Kaiden was his abandoned shotgun and a shivering clone.

Darwin's Angst

Yes, we can—
redesign them; make them grow
and develop according to your fantasies,
splicing DNA like reels of film noir
in the cutting room at Warner Bros.
where they made James Cagney walk on water
emptying the drum of his trench broom
into the halls of congress, bankers, gentlemen
before the land dropped out of Hollywood
and the Hays Code ruled over it all.

Yes, we can clone you—
ears, hearts, hands on the hunchbacks
and hindquarters of white laboratory mice
who (tenors all, and fearless) sing that aria
from *Cosi fan tutte* as a bat-winged Jean Harlowe
laughs and harvests their organs, their body parts
for yours and the international market
while Edward G. Robinson looks on, Godlike
in blue velvet pantaloons. Austere, approving.
Sane and wise as a man three days drunk on ether.

Ask us for something new and we will tell you
to build up your dreams, a name spelled out on a hill
not to be imagined but to be outdone
with what's at hand.   This primal stuff—
ourselves, corrupt as we are
and damaged goods. Now let all of the lights go out
in the haunted theater. Let the curtain fall
and throw a pall of dust over the parts we played
on this stage. For what purpose, and whose audience
we did not, and could not, know.

— W.C. Roberts

Bath Salts and Bedlam

Story by
Lyn McConchie

Illustration by
Neil T. Foster

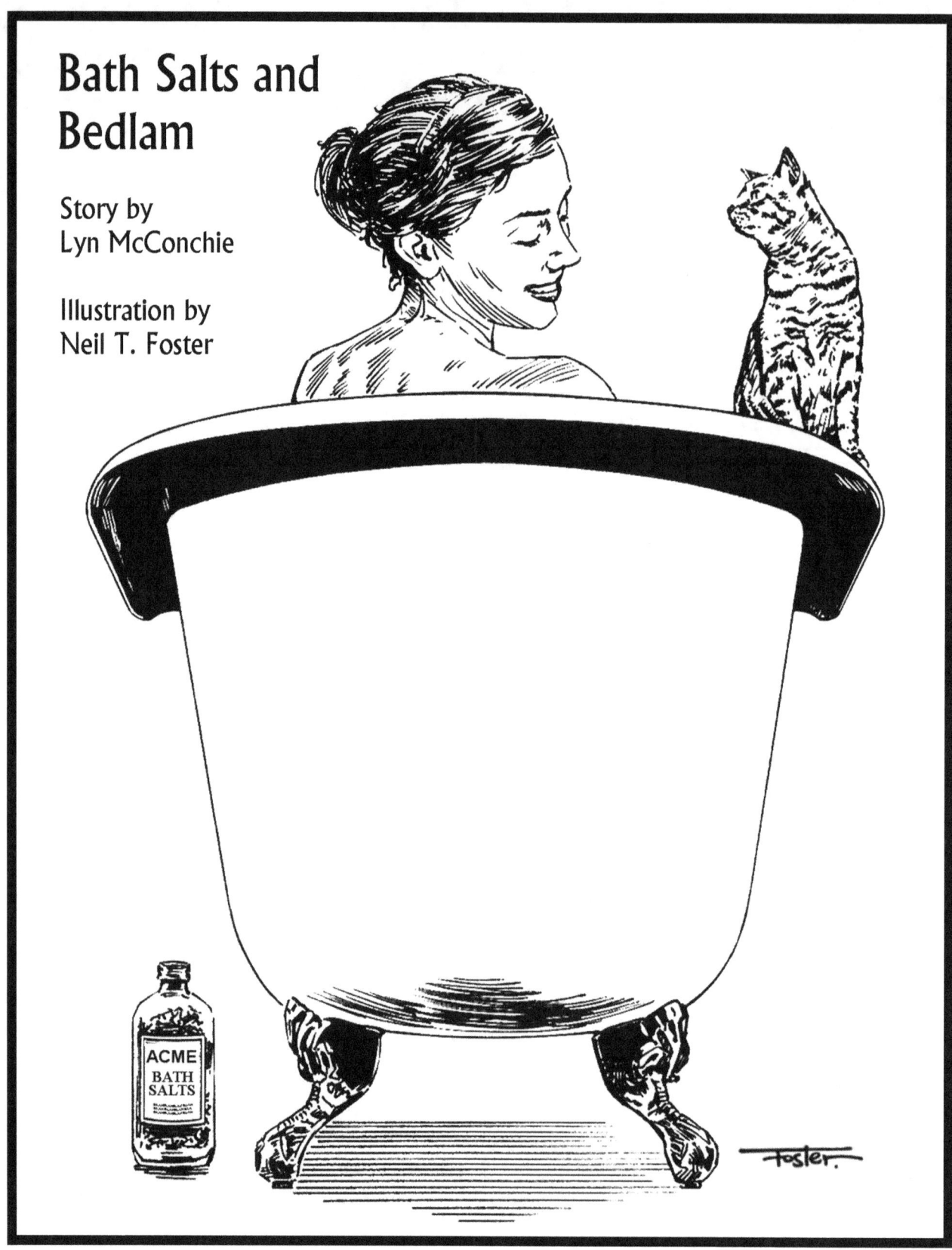

ACME
BATH
SALTS

Our local senior constable was here again today asking if I'd seen some missing bloke I could have *sworn* he said was named Bob Jonquil. I didn't take it the wrong way, I'd seen Joe coming from my neighbours' farm and watched as he went on to my other neighbour after I assured him I hadn't seen any man at all on my property this week whether he was named Bob Jonquil or Merriweather Anstruther Daffodil. My neighbours would have been saying they hadn't seen this Jonquil guy either. That's because I knew where he was, not that I'd actually seen him, but I knew all the same…

It all started with my new bath salts. I have a damaged leg, from a motorbike accident when I was thirty, and there's nothing that keeps me pain-free like a good long soak in very hot water before I go to bed. My old farmhouse bathroom has one of those long deep cast-iron claw-footed baths that's absolute bliss to lie back in when it's filled with hot water, and I do, regularly. And for a good soak you can't beat bath salts. About a year back a shop had opened up temporarily in our nearest township. It sold the tail ends of closing sales, over-runs of stock, goods turned back because they weren't quite to specifications and a stack of items like that.

One of the things they had was bath salts. The man running the shop had brought out a few bottles as I walked in the door and I looked them over. They were an odd shade of blue-green, and from the contents list on the back they were mostly made from Epsom salts and 'herbal additives', whatever those were, since they weren't listed beyond that, but the stuff smelled pleasant, and I bought a couple of bottles. Once I'd paid, the chap behind the counter cornered me away from other customers.

"I can see you're a lady who knows good merchandise when you see it."

I did, but that didn't mean I didn't see *him* for what he was. A con artist if ever I'd known one. I waited.

"Them bath salts, lady, they're the good stuff alright. S' just the colour puts people off. But I can do you a hell of a good deal. Gotta a case of it, another thirty-four bottles like the ones you bought, sell them to ya for an all in price?"

I considered. "How much?"

He named it and I kept my face from showing surprise. That *was* a good price and spread over thirty-four bottles it ended up around a fifth of what I'd pay for that amount of anything of even reasonable quality. It could be the whole consignment, three

dozen bottles counting the two already bought, and it made sense if he could sell them all for a single price.

"Just one thing, lady." I nodded that I was listening. "You don't want yer dog drinking the stuff, it don't go well with them."

I saw no need to go into long-winded explanations as to why I didn't have a dog. I merely said I'd be very careful and paid for the case, which he carried out to my old jeep.

I stayed the night with a friend whose husband was away on business and when I drove by the shop in the morning it was empty, all the merchandise apparently sold and the vendor gone. There had been a lot of people in there so I wasn't much surprised.

After that I went home, arriving at my farm gate to a raucous greeting from the geese.

I bought two geese twenty-five years ago, just after I purchased my farm. Every so often they raise another gosling, it joins the gaggle, and over the years the numbers have seesawed as goslings arrive and now and again something gets one of the adults. It's been steady on six adults for a couple of years now and that suits me. I lost one some time back when an intruder kicked one of the older geese to death. I think the gaggle mourned her, she'd been the matriarch, and I have to say I wasn't that happy about it either.

I got the original pair as watch-geese, and they do—watch, that is. Anyone they don't know sets foot on the property and they scream like something on the rack. After dark, and even if they know the intruder they still scream. And while usually it's all noise, if they have goslings or eggs or are feeling territorial, it can turn very nasty. I'd only had the place a year when burglars targeted my sheds; they left, not so much running as low flying—unlike their pursuers—with the geese hot on their heels. (My geese are Sebastopols, they're big strong birds, but they can't fly, which is convenient since I don't have to worry about clipping their wings, but they certainly can run if they need to.)

I opened the gate and greeted them. "Okay, okay, I'll feed everybody as soon as I get the jeep put away." I did, and while they were busy I managed to haul the case of bath salts out and get it inside, using the small trolley I normally employed for sacks of feed. I opened the case again, stacked the bottles on a shelf in the bathroom linen cupboard, and took the carton outside. It'd get used; everything does around here, sooner or later. Then I looked at the time and nodded. I could put dinner on and have a bath while it cooked.

I ran the bath, added a generous amount of

bath salts, climbed in and relaxed. The salts smelled great, and I could feel the heat soaking through my dud leg. The cat wandered in, leaned over and took a mouthful of bath water.

"Oi, Fluffy, get out of that." But then, the bloke hadn't said I shouldn't let the cat drink the stuff, just about dogs, so probably it was okay. I climbed out, dried off, dropped a caftan over my head and went to eat dinner.

Things were quiet for weeks after that until the bathroom waste pipe broke, the one that drained the bath water into my septic tank. I'd let the sheep onto the lawn to eat the grass down and one of the lambs—there's always one—had jumped on the pipe and broken it. So now the bath water ran into the small hollow by the drain instead of down it. I didn't worry much, in fact it was probably good, I wouldn't need to get the tank emptied for a lot longer and believe me, when you live out in the country getting that done costs a bomb, so I left it be. I noticed the geese drinking now and again after I let the bath empty, and now and again the cat took a drink too, but that was okay, and everything was fine.

About six months after that I heard the geese yelling one night. They quieted down pretty quickly though and I went back to sleep. In the morning I checked the sheds, and one of the doors was ajar. I figured some idiot had been sneaking around to see if there was anything he could steal and the geese had seen him off. Nothing unusual about that. Our village is between two bigger towns and it's surprising how often some little yob thinks it'd be fun to take a drive into the country and see what's portable.

That was why I got geese in the first place. You don't have to register them, they cost less to feed, and if they bite someone you can't be charged with an offence. Cops don't expect you to control geese. They're more effective than a dog too, I can't count how many times I've seen some big burly truck-driver back away when the gaggle advance. It's their beaks, snapping at just the right level to intimidate that does it. I don't have any trouble with them, they know me and I know them, and before now I've helped an injured one so they trust me and I suppose you get fond of someone who feeds you too.

They were in full cry again a few weeks later, same as last time they went quiet again after a minute or two and I went back to sleep. It happened again a month after that and I was getting annoyed, next time I'd get up, and if I saw whoever it was I'd have something to say to them. It was the week after that

when I noticed an item in the newspaper, nothing much, just a couple of brief paragraphs saying that three men from the big town four hour's drive to the north had gone missing. All three were known criminals so I'd bet no one was asking that many questions. I grinned, off on a spree most likely and they'd be back once they ran out of grog—probably surprised as all hell that the police had bothered to wonder about them.

Well, to cut a long story short, more petty crooks went missing, I kept getting woken up by the geese every month or so, and all that kept my leg from going mad about my walking about on it too much looking around, was that hot bath and those bath salts. And then I had another burglar when I was already awake. It was almost one a.m. and I'd been watching TV. I'd turned it off, made myself a hot chocolate and I heard the gaggle start to scream just as I put down my empty mug on the kitchen table by the door.

I scooped up the old cavalry sabre I keep handy and I was outside before the first yell died away. "Okay, who's there? Whaddaya up to?"

There was a sort of squeal, a thrashing, and something was floundering on the ground, the geese closed in and the thrashing stopped. I flicked my torch in that direction. Then I went back inside and shut the door. I have a good imagination but I know when something is that and when it isn't. That hadn't been. I waited until daylight, went out to feed the geese and noticed they didn't seem to be hungry. Thinking back they hadn't been hungry after each night there'd been a commotion. And that's when I knew for sure I hadn't imagined what I'd seen.

I waited until the next day and this time when I fed them I did it by hand. They came up one by one, took the wheat gently from my palm as they always had but this time I reached out and carefully moved their heads so that I got a look inside each beak. Wow! That explained the missing burglars and the gaggle's lack of interest in breakfast the next day. I thought about things over the next week and decided to say nothing. My friends don't come sneaking around my farm in the early hours, and if for some reason they needed to, they'd phone in advance.

I couldn't see that the area was any poorer for the loss of a sprinkling of petty crooks either. So there it was. I'd leave well enough alone, and I did. Over the weeks following I heard the geese tune up a time or two and stayed in the house, wondering as I listened what had caused their change? And as I soaked in the bath one evening, the water dyed that odd shade of blue-green, I looked down—and two and two suddenly made nine. The bath salts!

The seller had said to keep my dog away from them, maybe what he'd *really* meant, was 'all animals'? I asked about very quietly to see if I could find the man who'd run the shop, but he was nowhere to be found and no one knew anything about him. In fact it looked as if he may not have even had the right to set up there. Where had the bath salts come from and what exactly were the claimed 'herbal additives'? What did they do to a bird or animal that drank enough of them and was any change permanent? Could whatever drank the stuff control the change or was it random?

Sixteen days later I had an insight into that when I saw the cat hypnotise a mouse into coming out of hiding and walking right into the cat's jaws. It looked as if the change was geared to what the animal wanted. The geese hadn't liked their matriarch kicked to death in front of them, so maybe they'd wanted a way to make sure it didn't happen again? And the cat wanted an easy way to catch prey.

What else could have drunk the wastewater? It would only have been my cat inside, and outside the geese were usually around the hollow the moment they heard the water running out. It had taken months of regular drinking to make the changes. At least one bottle, maybe two.

And then I remembered. I'd given two bottles of the bath salts to my friend with whom I'd stayed the night after that day in town. She led a miserable life with a husband who knocked her around, usually after he got back from a business trip, and he ill-treated her big gentle greyhound as well. Andrea adored that dog and it adored her. And I wondered, (the man had specifically mentioned not allowing a dog to drink bath-salted water) if Smidge had been drinking the bath water, (and that is something house dogs often do) just what change would Andrea's dog wish for—and, how long would it take before we found out?

Finding Aliens

Starflight so stubbornly
Not a practical option
Project Ozma's radio-ears
So full of silence from the skies—
Some scientists now see test-tubes
As our only hope.

Create life.

It will be alien.

— Ruth Berman

Sacrifice

Story by
Carma Lynn Park

Illustration by
Jag Lall

She manifested but once a year, to grant petitions and to take the sacrifice. Now, perched on her god-throne, she gazed at the preparations with one multi-faceted eye, then the other. One of her priests moved around the shrine lighting the lamps. The flames' reflections shivered in the slick black marble walls. Other priests filled blue-glazed bowls with water and floated flowers in them. She approved of their quiet, respectful movements, their bowed heads.

When the preparations were completed, they slowly pushed open the double bronze doors twice their height, so heavy the priests had to lean into them.

Eight supplicants had gathered in the outer courtyard and had been dressed in clean white linen robes. The year before, only one had dared to make a petition.

She would take only one to be the sacrifice, but all who offered themselves would have their petitions fulfilled, simply because they were willing to hazard their lives.

When the doors were open and the prayer-bells shaken, priests shepherded the supplicants into the shrine. Some stumbled on two fear-frozen legs; others sagged and could hardly walk at all. They stopped partway to the throne, huddled together as if for safety.

The priests began their prayer-chants, but already she hungered, and moved restlessly, chitinous legs ticking against the pewter legs of the throne. When the prayers ended, she descended from the throne, first the head and heavy, serrated forelegs, then the twiggy middle and back legs.

She stalked toward the supplicants, who leaned away from her, trembling. Their sweat stank of fear. Tears slipped down one woman's face, but she didn't seem to notice them, eyes wide and staring at the god. The supplicants didn't look at each other; all of their attention was pinned on the god.

Most wore a bag on a flax cord around their neck, stuffed with thin paper closely written with prayers, and the bag rose and fell with their jagged breathing. Amused, the god noted that one man wore a moonstone carved with the head of the falcon god, to ward away evil. A woman had rubbed her body with bitter-smelling herbs, hoping to make herself unappealing. A thickset man had decorated his arms and legs with henna, interweaving signs for good fortune—pointed waves signifying the mother river; the turtle for long life; folded hands. A man's lips were moving soundlessly, but the god read, "Don't take me,

don't take me, don't take me." That was what they all wished, of course, that she would take someone else.

The man who petitioned alone last year had worn a prayer bag but no amulets or decorations. His face had been pale as clay, and his breath had come in gasps, but his steps were firm as they took him to her throne.

Now, as she circled the eight supplicants, the god descried their petitions in their minds: for generous crops after three years of barren fields, to keep the family from starving; for the sickness in his lungs to be healed so he could be strong again and not have to beg for handouts; for a husband to be brought home safely from battle; for a healthy baby, not one that struggled its way out of the womb only to sicken and die.

The man with the amulet dashed for the doorway, tripped with his own speed, and fell sprawling on the marble floor, then scuttled out on hands and feet. No one tried to stop him. His petition would go unfulfilled.

The god paused in front of a woman whose legs gave way, and she sank to the floor, covering her face with her hands. Lust and jealousy boiled in her. She wanted her friend to die so that she could have the husband. The god's jaw clicked sideways, and she hissed, "Take her away." Two priests hauled her to her feet and led her out between the bronze doors. Her petition would go unfulfilled.

Only six remained. Each looked at the others, realizing their odds had just narrowed from one in eight to one in six.

Any one of them would make a suitable sacrifice, and she was hungry. Her two front legs shot out and seized the thickset man. A choked, thin whimper. Her mandibles crunched through the neck. The body went limp and heavy as she dragged it to the throne for her god-meal.

The year before, the lone supplicant had knelt in front of her throne and bowed his head, baring the nape of his neck. Slowly, reluctantly, she had descended from the throne to inspect him.

There are imperatives even a god must obey. Finally she had hissed, "Your son will be well," before accepting his life. But she tasted no flesh and lapped no blood. Instead she had turned away and told the priests, "Take the body to his family."

Colby and the Holies

Story by Douglas Empringham
Illustration by Jag Lall

1 - Carpenters

The fog had reached ground level, leaving Colby to rely more on his preternatural hearing than his enhanced night vision. He heard someone approaching on soft-soled shoes. When they met under a street lamp, she sent him a wry smile and said:

"Ah, petite Colby. Fortune's pet."

It seems Gloriana has abandoned her Goth look. She was tricked out in the togs of an old-time stage magician. Gravity had not caused her features to sag more than he remembered while she now had the complexion of an arsenic eater. She too was outside time. "Did that poser Bugiardo finally made good on his promise?"

"No. As many warned me, I was abandoned at the gate, one bite short of the promised land. It was Lady Voile who fulfilled my—"

Hearing a release of tension and fearing a crossbow, Colby sprang toward a vacant shop's doorway. Behind him a spinning circular saw blade was parting Gloriana from her head.

So much for Holy Carpenters being a paranoid fantasy!

He forced the door and took refuge within. The shop, stripped of fixtures, had both a door to the alley and a stair to rooms above. He opted for the latter.

From a room above he watched three figures gather about the fallen Gloriana. All wore goggles with tinted lenses, gauntlets, heavy bib aprons with deep pockets, and work boots. One had a device strapped to his wrist that combined a crossbow and a 45 rpm turntable. This apparently launched the decapitating saw blade and was now being fitted with another. A small disk having many teeth, And probably, he thought, diamond tipped.

The other two carpenters were armed with older tools: an adze and a maul and wedges. The second also had an iron-strapped mallet hanging from a belt loop.

"And the kid?" asked Ms. Maul & Wedges.

"Yeh," sneered Mr. Adze. "Punk oughta thank us for savin' him from that lamia."

"Too swift to be human," said Mr. Blade-slinger, "even if he's a runt."

As Colby was but 59 1/2 inches tall, slender, and had the visage of a greeting card angel, his age was regularly pegged at fourteen or less.

"She prob'ly *turned* him," said Mr. Adze, stroking the thin blade of his shaping tool.

The leader had used his cellphone, and a black van now arrived with the side door sliding open.

Gloriana's parts were promptly reunited inside a plastic bag then tossed inside.

In another room Colby found a window overlooking the fire escape. As he opened it, the black van entered the alley below—and he heard running footsteps on the roof above. He was hedged in if not yet hopelessly trapped.

A tour of the barren rooms yielded nothing useful. There was a mirror, but that wasn't something a vampire could use to create an illusion. In the next moment he detected the faint squeak of a stair tread.

Colby went to the larger room, sprang atop of the door, and balanced on the molding above. The carpenter advanced softly, holding his breath, staying close to the wall. Before entering, he sent the beam of brilliant light into the room—which also illuminated the pistol crossbow in his other hand. Loaded, he presumed, with a wooden bolt having an iron core.

As his enemy passed below, Colby dropped onto his shoulders and jerked his head violently from side to side. And as the carpenter's spine snapped, the crossbow discharged its lethal dart. Colby then rode the collapsing body to the floor, where he took possession of both weapon and flashlight, which he switched off.

While he spanned and reloaded the crossbow, the sound of glass bursting came from the stairs. The first of many holy water grenades, he soon realized.

They are hoping to drive me onto the fire escape…

He wanted to answer by shooting an arrow down the stairwell, but just then a phial caromed and shattered close to him, causing him to retreat.

Colby then recalled seeing a telephone line outside a window, one that was casement rather than sash. When he opened this noiselessly, he observed that the line was old and frayed. It would pull loose from the insulator without undo exertion.

A last resort. Who knows how many are lurking outside?

He did not trouble to speculate, not with ground level fog and gusts of wind creating moving shadows.

Then a whiff of tobacco smoke came from the street directly below. The holy water grenadier had stepped outside for a cigarette before hazarding the stair.

Colby braced himself and leaned out—just as the carpenter moved away from the storefront to toss their cigarette into the gutter. At that he gleefully let fly with a bolt, even as the carpenter sensed him, turned, and looked up. Thus taking the arrow in his throat.

As the smoker flopped to the sidewalk, he discharged a saw blade that skipped and whirled across to the opposite curb. Raising an echoing clatter surely heard for blocks.

He might have used the line then in hopes of gaining the lethal blade launcher, but the carpenters reacted too quickly. Within seconds the black van came skidding to a halt. The driver and another jumped out and were met by two more Holy Carpenters. But while the four blustered with fury their movements were wary and tentative.

Because none took note of the angle at which the bolt had penetrated, no one looked up. One relieved their fallen comrade of the blade-slinging harness and strapped it on, then the four crept into the store. Not an opportunity Colby could pass up. But he waited until he heard them crunching broken glass on the stair before he sprang to the sill, seized the phone line—which pulled free with ease—and swung down beside the van. And not only was the key in the ignition, the engine was still running.

Away sped the now merry vampire, his enemies reduced to diminishing figures gesturing frantically in a side-view mirror.

2 - Fishers

Having escaped the Holy Carpenters, Colby abandoned their van near the Golden Gate bridge. Not being a traditionalist, instead of transforming into a bat he levitated and glided under the bridge and around the Marin headlands. It wasn't that he had a particular dislike of the opera *Der Fledermaus*, he simply preferred to kite. Though rarely so high as to appear on radarscopes. (A necessary precaution in the Age of Paranoia.)

His destination was a derelict cemetery and a ruined mansion north of Mount Tamalpais. But on arriving he saw there had been changes in the five years since his last stay. The crypts and mausoleums had been cleaned of grime and graffiti, the headstones were now upright, and the paths weeded and neatly paved with black pebbles.

When he hovered and gazed west, he had just enough moon—and starlight to see that the mansion had also been restored to its former glory. And by his kind, as illumination came from candles and ultraviolet lamps.

His curiosity roused, he glided as far as the garden. Which was now given over entirely to roses. Surrounding the gazebo there were tea roses, a favorite.

Nearer the house a pair of wolves came sprinting toward him—not that they were any sort of threat. They instantly yielded to his will and followed at his heels.

As Colby approached the open French windows, he glimpsed an interior aggressively overdone in the Victorian manner. This household was decidedly orthodox Undead. (Whereas his taste favored the more refined and restrained Louis Quinze.)

A tall and regally cadaverous man appeared in the doorway. One wearing an opera cape over a starched shirtfront and eveningwear. He offered no welcome and viewed Colby closely through a quizzing-glass before saying:

"Scruffy in extremis."

Colby freely admitted that his pale jeans and Henley shirt could use a wash. Instead of feeling self-conscious, he parried, "Mine is a vigorous and often harried life."

"There is no welcome here for runaways or castaways."

"I came for the moonlight badminton contest."

"Poppycock."

"I prefer playing with a shuttlecock."

Showing the faintest of smiles, the other asked, "What did you hope to find here?"

"Asylum."

"I suppose you mean sanctuary."

"I say asylum, you say sanctuary."

"From who or what?"

"The Holy Carpenters."

"Yet another folk legend?"

"A bit more substantial. Think of a mechanical device that can hurl circular saw blades as if they were ninja throwing stars. I witnessed a Holy Carpenter decapitate one of ours. Barely escaped myself."

"Saw blades? How mortal and lacking in finesse. I shall make inquiries." The other was poised to shut the door then changed his mind and commented, "I remarked your arrival. Do you have a particular dislike of taking bat form? I happen to be quite traditional myself."

"Those who choose to levitate need not worry about flying cats."

The smile became marginally less faint but more arch. "If I have your word you will do nothing to discomfort the guests soon to arrive, you may rest in one of the mausoleums."

"Less than ideal hospitality," Colby said, with a small bow, "but courteous enough to be appreciated. Thank you."

"Another time, wearing more suitable attire, you might be invited to enter."

How curious am I? he wondered, strolling away. The wolves escorted him to the edge of the lawn then trotted back to their master.

He considered the temple-like tombs with Doric columns but chose a limestone crypt paneled in lacquered bamboo. The faint light was enough for him to appreciate an interior done in tasteful arterial red. There was also an altar, though it lacked an idol or offerings. The ancestral couple interred here, he decided, were either of Asian extraction or particularly fond of that part of the world.

* * *

Colby was pondering his next destination when he heard subdued voices outside. Which proved to be two people wearing black face paint, dusters, jumpsuits and shoes. They were perched upon tombstones and studying the mansion through monoculars.

"Another bat crossing the moon," said the nearer one, speaking into a cellphone.

"The bat is now a female bloodsucker," added the other, in a lighter voice. "If you care, she is wearing … looks like dark taffeta with pale lace."

He was relieved to notice no carpenter's gear.

But they could be another gang of vampire-hunters.

The taller asked his companion to keep watch while he, fitting a silencer to an automatic, went to "take out the wolves."

Colby checked an impulse to fly and warn those in the house. What he needed to know first was: how many were there? *And,* what other weapons did they have? (Handguns did little more than annoy the Undead.)

He made a silent approach on the remaining sentinel. "So you know they've wolves on guard," he said, sotto voce.

The other (female by her odor and profile silhouette), though startled, instantly recovered. Then she studied him with such intensity that she became easy prey to a mesmeric spell. Which freed Colby to help himself to a sanguine snack while she watched the mansion.

Which proved to be a disappointment. He had hoped for a devotee of junk food, a diet that added to the blood's toothsomeness. She was a vegan.

"Does your team have a name?" he asked.

She nodded and showed him an intaglio medallion depicting a fisherman casting a net. The legend read: Holy Fisher.

Another self-sanctified posse!

"Do you know the Holy Carpenters?"

She gave him a blank look just as her cellphone barked: "Net time!"

Colby followed like a shadow during her charge down the slope, not even pausing to view the two dead wolves. But nearer the house he turned aside. A window had opened and a vampire emerged in the act of taking bat form. Only to be enveloped in a casting net thrown from behind.

Even as the Undead struggled the web liquefied. Colby watched in horrified disbelief as the bat decomposed at a wildly accelerated rate. Soon, too impossibly soon, naught remained but wisps of rust-colored mist, that in turn vanished.

Un*holy Fishers!*

Elsewhere vampires sought to escape by transforming into swarms of flies. These too were trapped in nets they were unable to pass through. Maggot flies that ignited, shone brighter than fireflies for an instant, then expired without leaving a trace of residue.

Colby was kept from fleeing by a surge of anger. While victorious Holy Fishers stormed into the mansion celebrating their defeat of "Lucifer bugs," he overtook and overcame one, taking his a pistol and life. He then circled the house in maximum stealth mode, intolerably aware of the lethal nets in play.

Presently the Holy Fishers separated in quest of loot, enabling Colby to pick them off. And every one was so caught off guard that none went for a net instead of a sidearm. Reducing themselves to clichéd fish in a barrel.

In addition to reloading and acquiring a second pistol, Colby emptied the master bedroom dresser of cash and gold jewelry. (Being kith if not kin, he felt entitled.)

When he calculated that the last three were at the bar in the salon, he surprised them in the middle of a toast. And quickly introduced two to Death. The third managed to slide down behind the bar.

Crouching there, he called: "Izzy, use your net! I'm all out!"

The girl from the cemetery appeared and hovered just inside the French doors, a picture of indecision.

The man shouted, "Then throw it to me, you stupid bitch!"

Colby charged the bar during this. His first shot missed but the next went through the man's ear as he scrambled to the far end of the bar, all the while swearing ferociously.

She stared at Colby. In the excitement of the raid she had overcome being his thrall, Now, in a shock of recognition, she worked out that he was one of Them!

"Remember me from the graveyard?" he asked.

"You could shoot me easy…"

"I don't have a reason." Yet.

Her jaw worked silently till at last she managed a crooked smile. "My name is Isabelle. I keep asking that stupid bastard to stop calling me Izzy!" With a laugh that was also a snort, she moved closer to the man while pulling a net from a plastic cone.

"Where did your … club get those nasty toys?"

Instead of answering, she said, "Lumpy's not my step-father anymore, thanks to you. I owe you." She dropped the net over the corpse and settled on a bar stool to watch. After a long minute she told him:

"Lumpy's a chemist, a bio-chemist. He invented the nets. His 'big score' that was gonna make him rich. Not that he'd share with my mom and me. He was only generous with himself."

"'Who did he think would pay so much for his nets?"

Her mind was elsewhere. "I feel so awesomely happy!" she cried, doing a wobbly pirouette. "He's gone, just like I wished! Can't never come back—no matter what mom wants!"

"Hoisted on his own petard. Or … on whatever he calls those nets."

Now she answered him: "Easy money webs. There's a disk on the cord. You press it and a current mixes the chemicals in the filaments. They work like maggots on meth."

A deep chill caught up with him, the reaction he'd been neatly avoiding. What he'd seen was not a memory he could easily forget.

"These guys are from a drug cartel," She meant the two men who'd been drinking with her step-father. "After a way to get *totally* rid of enemies and guys who know too much."

Here's who Lumpy thought would make him rich.

"Did he start the vampire-hunter group?"

"No. That was me and my friends. He only got serious about vampires after the cartel guys came. That's who found out about this place. Before, we just brought Lumpy roadkill. And for once he wasn't stingy."

"But now you are a true believer." He kept his smile thin and wry.

In return she laughed and told him, "Your gun's empty. I heard it click on empty after you snuffed Lumpy."

"True enough" He tossed the empty pistol aside then brought out the automatic with an extended clip. "But this one's full."

She responded by drawing her own and shooting from the hip. A bullet that struck him in the sternum and made him take a step back to regain his balance. She then tried to duck behind the bar only to get tangled in her step-father's jumpsuit. And in falling to her knees she let the weapon drop.

"I might be more or less invulnerable," Colby said, examining the hole in his shirt, "but my wardrobe doesn't have that advantage."

With eyes filled with dread, she pleaded, "Sorry—sorry! I … I had'a know if it was true. An'—an' it's more than awesome…!"

Instead of letting his finger squeeze the trigger, he listened to a reason against. "I'll let you square the account by flushing all the remaining nets." He wanted them out of existence!

"Deal!" She was immediately up and searching the bodies for the tapering plastic cones. "I think you're a guy first and then a vampire."

"What made you want to be a Holy Fisher?" he asked, as he followed and watched.

"It started out as a church group."

"What principle did you rally around? Vampires are evil?"

"Yeah, mos'ly. But also … umm, once you're dead you ought'a stay dead."

"As your step-father will stay."

"Him being gone is already a happy place for me."

Which is how Colby felt about seeing nets vanish in surges of water. But he was not so overcome with joy that he missed her holding back a cone and slipping it up her sleeve.

"And if mom and me cash in on Lumpy's 'Big Score,' she'd get the condo she wants and I'd get my own car."

"Aren't you forgetting what interests the cartel? Sure, they'd offer you a pile of money. And take away Lumpy's chemicals and papers. But then? "

The face under the sooty makeup, a wide one with a small thin nose and mouth, had been mulish. Now it was dipping into sullen.

"Why don't you take another look at Lumpy, *Isabelle of the nets?*"

"I know, okay? I know!" she cried, stamping her foot.

"I can understand your being tempted. Lots of people think drug money is free money. But if you made a deal with them, you'd become someone who knew too much. A bullet would settle that, a net and you'd be gone completely."

"When was las' time you met up with somethin' scary as our nets?" she asked, with a sly smile. "Mus' be freakin' weird."

"Do yourself a favor. When someone comes asking about Lumpy, tell them he packed his lab and hit the road. The cartel will believe—"

"Yeah, okay. Like you say, They'll think he's out shoppin' for a sweeter deal!" The enthusiasm behind her words was almost real. But before a minute could pass, as she turned away, her shadow revealed that she was tugging something from her sleeve. His bullet stopped her before she could pivot and cast.

Watching the net feast on her, Colby resolved to seek out and destroy all facts concerning Lumpy's sinister creation. If he could manage that, there would be no peril to warn or convince others about. (Though he doubted he'd ever feel quite the same about nets.)

On Halloween Night

It's Halloween Night, when all's a'fright,
with witches and goblins and ghosts about.

The ghouls are grinning, vampires are drinking,
while little ones scurry for treats to eat.

Then cupboards run bare, and there's many a scare,
for those who aren't quick receive a little trick.

But we mustn't forget the Evens of yore,
when Jack took his lantern out on the moor.

And Druids presided at esoteric rites,
to save the world from a long, lengthening night.

— Gary W. Davis

The Fourth Setting

Story by Simon Bleaken
Illustration by Tom Kelly

Henders had that look in his eye, the one that always meant trouble. He had been pacing restlessly around the lab for the last half hour, ever since that curious envelope had arrived, and now he looked both agitated and excited in equal measure. A thin line of sweat beaded his creased brow beneath his swiftly receding hairline, and his upper lip was almost quivering. His gaze flicked nervously to the curious squat pillar of grey-green stone that sat amidst a sea of wires, cables and softly-humming monitoring devices; a stone that had been the sole consuming object of both his time and attention for weeks now.

"We're going to try the fourth setting," he announced in the tone of voice he always used for decisions that were not to be questioned.

From where he sat on the other side of the lab Tom McKenzie watched him uneasily as he flicked through the results from their earlier tests. He doubted that Henders had been eating or sleeping properly for days now—maybe even weeks judging by the bags under his eyes, the gauntness that had crept into his face, and the speed with which his frayed temper had been giving out, but he knew that no amount of argument on his part would do any good. The man could teach mules how to be stubborn.

"It's late," McKenzie commented, though he made no attempt to check his watch. Such a gesture was likely only to anger Henders and make him even more unreasonable. "We're the only ones still here. Shouldn't we wait until we have a full team back in tomorrow?"

"Science doesn't sleep."

"No, but people do."

"We're close, McKenzie—close to understanding this ancient marvel that sits among us. I thought that you of all people would share in that passion, that dedication."

"I do—and I understand, this is important," McKenzie ventured tactfully. "But I've got a wife and a two-year old kid at home. I've got to think of them as well."

"You are. With the work we're doing here, you're putting food on their table and paying off that new television set, and you're also helping make their world a safer place. And tonight, while they sleep soundly, you and I are going to try the fourth setting."

"We got those bad power spikes on the third setting—dangerous ones, remember?" he reminded Henders cautiously. "With the levels of energy that rock is emitting, who knows what might happen?"

"What's your point?" Henders narrowed his eyes as he shot a fierce glare at McKenzie.

"Have I really got to spell it out?"

"If you have concerns or doubts, then enlighten me," Henders said testily.

"This rock defies everything we know. Not only is it a mystery to every geologist we've consulted, it also appears to be *generating* energy, and seems to respond to us by increasing its output to levels that shouldn't be possible. Yet it's not magnetic or radio-active, has no surface temperature, and as far as we can determine there are no discernible electrostatic charges present within it at all. Nothing that should allow it to do what it has been doing. I just think we should stop and go over the findings very thoroughly before—"

Henders shot him a look that could have melted steel, furious that anyone dared question his decision. "Caution is for those who have time."

"With all due respect, we've all the time in the world."

"Is that so?" Henders folded his arms, his gaze icy. "What if this isn't the only stone of its kind out there? We were lucky that a US archaeological team found this first and not a Russian one. Can you imagine if this got into the hands of the Commies? They've already started firing rockets and dogs into space—just think what they could do with a source of power like this!"

McKenzie fell silent and let his eyes return to the sheaf of papers he had been studying. He knew Henders had a point—the application for the rock went far beyond a potential source of limitless renewable energy. It would undoubtedly have endless applications for weapon's technology too. McKenzie's eyes returned to the manila envelope still sitting on the next desk, the one with the government stamp on the front and Henders' name in thick black print right under that, and he wondered for the hundredth time just what was in it. It had been hand-delivered that afternoon by a man in a dark suit that McKenzie had never seen around the labs before. But he recognised the stern unsmiling face of a government official when he saw one, and that's exactly what he had seen staring out from under the stranger's pristine black fedora. There was more going on here than Henders was telling, that much was certain, but McKenzie knew better than to try and press for information before Henders was ready to reveal it.

He just wished he knew more about the location where the rock had been discovered—supposedly some isolated little island somewhere in the South

Pacific Ocean. Word on the grapevine was that the local tribe apparently venerated the rock, claiming it had prophetic properties—supposedly giving glimpses of other worlds, places and times, and allowed them to commune in a dream-trance with their strange gods, all in return for blood offerings made atop the stone. There were wild tales of victims apparently flayed alive or garrotted while shamans with pierced faces carved bloody chunks out of them with a flint blade, before dressing in skinned strips of dripping flesh and dancing into a wild frenzy to the damnable pounding of tribal drums. And all that, allegedly, while the rest of the village chanted and screamed, as they cavorted and danced in a wild throng around the sacrificial stone. It sounded beyond barbaric, and were customs utterly unlike any found on the wholly peaceful neighbouring islands. Just the thought of it was enough to churn McKenzie's stomach. He had even heard claims that three of the expedition members had actually been slain just trying to smuggle the stone back to their boat. It was hard to believe things like that still happened now in 1959—it sounded more like something out of the dark ages.

"McKenzie?"

He blinked and realised he'd been drifting in thought—worse, he'd been staring right at the envelope. He looked up, face flushing. "Yes?"

"I said can you activate the electrical field?" Henders repeated again. If he had noticed McKenzie's interest in the envelope he gave no sign. "I'll monitor responses and calibrate from the second station."

"I want my objections noted," McKenzie said as he made his way over to the generator controls. Henders gave an irritable nod and wave of the hand, but McKenzie knew he was unlikely to actually bother noting down anything. With a silent sigh he seated himself before the console and activated the switch, taking the dial up to the midway point before the first setting. He could feel the familiar tingle as the electricity began to flow through the rock and watched as already the readout dials were showing triple what they should have been.

"Increase up to two," Henders called over.

"We need to cycle up slowly," McKenzie warned, "we have to give the equipment time to…"

"Increase to two," the order came again, the tone less pleasant.

"Increasing now," McKenzie muttered, shaking his head. There was a noticeable dip in the ceiling lights as the dial turned and more electricity was channelled through the stone. The needles were now spiking and dancing dangerously high, and McKenzie recalled the first time they had dared take the setting to this level and the alarm that had created among the lab staff—back then, only just a few weeks ago, the thought of doing what they planned to try tonight would have been unthinkable.

"Now proceed to three."

McKenzie opened his mouth to protest then closed it again, knowing it would fall on deaf ears. He twisted the dial all the way to three, his body tensing. Around them the air was filled with the crackle and spark of electricity, the background hiss of static and the hum of the machines as they drew on more and more power. A smell of heating solder and ozone assaulted their nostrils—along with a foul stench like burning rubber that was growing stronger by the second. Henders meanwhile stood like a statue, his gaze fixed intently on the dials before him, mouth parted just a fraction, and that obsessive twinkle sparkling in his eyes that reminded McKenzie of the look of a kid coming down to open the gifts around the tree on Christmas morning.

"We're at three now," McKenzie reported, casting a worried glance at the readings that were coming back in. "This doesn't look good."

"Understood. Hold it here for a second."

The lights fizzled and dipped overhead, and the burning smell was getting worse—more acrid. The dials on the console continued to spike, but hadn't gone into the red yet. Even so, McKenzie felt uneasy in his gut and wiped his sweating palms on his legs.

"Get ready to take it up to the fourth setting," Henders gestured excitedly, his hand trembling.

"Have you seen these readings?" McKenzie called over, "they look worse than last time."

"Everything's fine. I expected this."

"Seriously?"

"It's fine."

"We're about to blow half the equipment in here if we don't give it time to adjust. And even if we do, at these levels…"

"I reinforced the capacitors myself—they can take it."

"This is crazy—you'll get us both killed!"

"We must keep going. The key to unlocking the potential within the rock lies with the correct application of channelled energy. It is my belief we are dealing with more than a mere power source here, rather something created by a science yet unknown to us—but for what purpose? What reason?" he stared over at the stone, a half-smile crossing his face. "We shall soon discover its purpose. I know we are close to finding the truth."

"How can you know that? That's not science, that's conjecture."

"Educated conjecture based upon the evidence gathered so far," Henders said, waving the accusation away.

"So let's gather more—slowly, under more controlled conditions. Why are we rushing in like workmen with a sledgehammer? Science requires a finely-tuned and careful approach. You know that—or you used to. What's changed?"

"Time is of the essence."

"Why?" McKenzie demanded furiously. "Why all the sudden urgency to figure out this thing? What aren't you telling me?"

"Because—!" Henders snarled, then visibly reigned himself in before continuing, "there *is* another stone. The Russians have it."

McKenzie fell back onto his seat, all the arguments and warnings that had been about to leave his lips had fallen silent.

"Now you understand," Henders ran a shaking hand through his thin greying hair. "The government wants to know what we have here, and we're lucky they are letting us work on it. If we fail to get results, they'll take it to someone who can—our funding with it. But worse than that, if the maximum power output of this rock is even close to what I think it may be, then in the hands of the Russians—well, we won't stand a chance unless we possess that power too, or can unlock its secrets first. If we don't beat them to understanding what we have here, it could be the end of us all."

"I didn't know," McKenzie said softly, shaking his head.

"You weren't supposed to. Now you do. And I promise you, the Commies won't stop or worry about safety concerns. They'll do what it takes to unlock the secrets of that rock—and harness the true strength of its power. Now you see why we must press on?"

McKenzie nodded slowly, humbled and stunned. He reached for the dial, feeling the cold steel under the tips of his fingers as he swallowed dryly. "Ready for the fourth setting."

"We're making history tonight," Henders declared. "I know it."

With that, McKenzie turned the dial to the fourth setting.

The needles spiked and flickered as the power output increased dramatically. The stone was spitting out energy levels at a rate even greater than either of them had expected or thought possible. A shrill whine rose up over the rumbling of the capacitors as they struggled to deal with the increase and the acrid smell was becoming unbearable. McKenzie was sure something must be burning back inside one of the units. He could feel the sweat running down his face as the machines continued to heat up.

The squat pillar of rock sitting amidst the coils of wire gave no visible sign of the power that was now rippling out of it, invisible and incredible, and McKenzie found his gaze moving back to it, a mix of curiosity and awe filling him. But there was something else too—something more primal. It had taken him a few nights to work out what it was, it was so deeply buried in his subconscious, but now he understood. There was an unaccountable sense of dread and revulsion hanging about that stone—one that went beyond the violent and bloody past connected to it from the sacrifices. It was as though something in the core of his being wanted to recoil from it and run screaming from the room, or to tip it into the biggest pit he could find and shovel dirt onto it, to bury it from the world. He never would have said anything about this to Henders. He knew the old man would berate him for giving into foolish superstition and weak emotional fears, but still, there was something about that rock that was *wrong,* and on some instinctive level, he knew it. It was as if he could hear the tribal drums every time he looked at it, could see blood running down the rock and taste the coppery taint thickly in the air. And behind those drums and the shrill wailing of the wildly thrashing and dancing natives, behind all that blood and chaos and carnage … he could hear whispers, faint and unnerving, coming out of that rock. And the harder he strained, the more he leaned forward, heart hammering in his chest as he tried to listen to what those strange voices were saying, the more he thought they weren't really voices at all, at least not human ones.

A capacitor sparked and started to fail, snapping McKenzie's attention from the rock and back onto his readouts. Everything was pushing into the red, and if Henders had not overridden the safety shut-offs the night before, the systems would have deactivated automatically by now.

"This is too much," McKenzie warned. "We should power it back down and go over the readings we got tonight."

"Just a few seconds more!"

"I don't think the equipment will—"

As if finishing his sentence for him a spark burst out of the side of one of the consoles followed by a cloud of thick noxious smoke. McKenzie scrabbled for the nearest extinguisher and doused the now dead unit in dry powder. The other machines were also showing signs of succumbing to the overwhelming stress on their systems. Warning lights flashed and flickered and fans whirred as they struggled to cool the failing equipment.

"Recalibrate!" Henders screamed, his eyes wide as he watched the output register. "Look at it—look! The power levels are accelerating faster! These readings, they are truly—"

But that was the last thing McKenzie heard before the lab exploded.

The force of the blast lifted him up and slammed him backwards, catapulting him across a bench in a spray of heat, sparks and broken glass. He landed heavily, gasping as the air was punched from his lungs, ears ringing and his whole body dazed and shaking. For a second he couldn't move—could only lie stunned and blinking as the room around him shook.

When his world finally started to settle he eased himself up slowly, his head spinning and the coppery taste of blood flooding his mouth. His shirt had torn open at both elbows and one whole side of his body was screaming at him where he had landed on broken glass. As he sat up he realised he was missing a shoe. His shocked brain tried to work out what had happened, but everything was blurry. He blinked twice as he forced himself to stand shakily, then a wave of terror washed over him as his eyesight and mind came back into focus together.

Henders stood in the centre of the room, his body swaying as though he were drunk and the tattered and bloody remains of his lab coat fluttering out around him like ragged streamers. He might simply have been in shock, but McKenzie could see the tendrils that were now coming out of the pillar of rock—translucent stalks that coiled and flexed like flickering tentacles, but which were neither light, nor radiation, nor electricity, but some strange combination of all of these and more—and which had now attached themselves to the back of Henders' head like the strings on a puppet.

"Helloooooooo baby!" the Big Bopper crooned as the radio on the shelf across the lab sputtered and kicked into life. There was one of the strange electrical tendrils coiling about it too, and crazily McKenzie found himself starting to laugh, a shrill high-pitched wail as his nails dug into his palms.

"In other news, United Airlines Flight 736 has been reported … celebrating yesterday's Stanley cup victory by the Montreal Canadiens against the Boston Bruins in…" the radio announced randomly as it skipped through stations, before suddenly falling silent as it shorted out. The ghostly tentacle that had been running across it was now moving up the wall, exploring blindly.

Henders meanwhile was lurching and shambling across the floor like some badly controlled marionette, those tendrils flowing out behind him, writhing and crackling, even as his body began to scorch and wither, his skin visibly darkening as angry red welts erupted across it. The stench that filled the air reminded McKenzie crazily of the family barbecue he had attended just last week and he gagged.

"N'gal thul'sath!" Henders screamed, his voice breaking under the effort and the tendons in his neck sticking out like metal cables. He crashed clumsily against a bench, the flesh on his face melting like hot wax as his hair burst into flame. "Yugg'gai n'ashanna vor y'gth tok'l grrrraaa…"

His scorched fingers groped awkwardly at the scattered objects on the bench—pawing at toppled Bunsen burners and tripods and running unfeelingly through broken glass that tore at the skin. It appeared as though he was trying to examine or pick them up, but had forgotten how his hands worked.

"Yugg'gai n'vor ztsdrah Iukkoth d'zzkl…" he howled as he went.

His contorted face was still screaming that insane gibberish moments later when his eyes burst like exploding eggs. He slumped forward, toppling to the floor as the flames raced over his arms and legs before finally consuming him. The tendrils that had been connected with his head broke loose, writhing in the air like agitated serpents.

It took McKenzie a good ten seconds to break through the paralysis of shock that held him rooted to the spot, staring at the blazing remains that lay crumpled just a few feet before him. But the smoke that was filling the air and the searing heat from the wrecked equipment soon jarred him back, and he dropped low to the ground, seeking breathable air, as he crawled painfully toward where he knew the nearest extinguisher would be. The floor was strewn with broken glass and debris and the air overhead was swiftly filling with noxious fumes. Even down close to the floor McKenzie found himself coughing and blinking back tears as his eyes began to sting and his lungs encountered the toxic smoke. He fumbled almost blindly past the main bench and then his fingers found the wall and stretched up into the haze until they encountered the cold metal of an extinguisher.

He snatched it down, angled the nozzle, then stood and frantically aimed it at the heart of the glow, holding his breath and blinking to try and focus his blurred vision. His eyes already felt like they were being peeled in their sockets, his cheeks were wet with tears and his lungs were now burning with the need to breathe. The kick from the extinguisher took him by surprise and he almost dropped it on his foot. As the cold blast of powder burst forth and doused the flaming equipment the roar it made deafened him. He turned quickly, trying to cover all of the flames, including the still-burning remains of Henders, when the whole extinguisher was ripped from his grip and lifted up into the air. He took a startled step back, colliding with a lab stool, and looked up. Through the swirling haze of fumes and smoke he saw one of the strange tendrils flexing and moving. He had almost forgotten about them in the panic. It had scooped up the extinguisher and was now examining it, turning it this way and that, almost like a child examining a new toy. Then it hurled the extinguisher aside and McKenzie threw himself to the floor as it tore through the air where his head had been moments before. He sat up, coughing and gasping, and that was when he finally noticed what was happening to the pillar of rock they had been studying. One of the machines had survived the explosion and was still channelling power into it, and whole sections of the pillar seemed to be liquefying in response—flowing down onto the floor in a molten state and pooling around the base. In the newly exposed sections he saw curious nubs of grey crystal and strange grooves, shaped in regular clusters of three, around each nub. But what caught his gaze most of all was the unaccountable mass of pale fleshy material that appeared to be pulsing like some kind of obscene heart in the centre of that slab of stone.

Then a sharp tingle, like pins and needles, ran along his leg as a tendril closed around his ankle. He felt the hairs on his whole body stand on end as a strange electrical charge flowed through him. He tried to snatch his leg away, but the tendril coiled up further, wrapping around his calf and tightening painfully around his thigh. A cry of alarm escaped him as he kicked and thrashed, trying to free his trapped limb—but the ghostly tentacle was lifting up now, carrying him with it. Desperately he grabbed at the

corner of one of the lab benches, anchoring himself, but his legs were being pulled closer to the pillar and it was taking all of his strength to hold on and keep the rest of him from following along with them.

Flexing translucent feelers were now emerging from the ends of each of the exposed crystal nubs on the pillar, reminding McKenzie of some sea anemones he had once observed, and he watched with growing panic as they gently probed his feet and ankles, running across the smooth leather of his shoe and the torn cloth of his trouser leg. Then one of them penetrated that thin layer of material and sank into his flesh. The pain lanced white-hot through his body and his arms and limbs convulsed painfully, his eyes bulged wildly in their sockets and his teeth clamped together. He couldn't scream, couldn't move, and the agony burned through him even as more of those flexing feelers penetrated his skin and began flowing up through his body, running underneath the flesh like spreading varicose veins.

The last remaining machine that was still channelling power now shorted out as the energy levels overwhelmed it. Thick black smoke belched from the side of the damaged console in plumes—and the warning glow of flames flared through the metal grating on the side as an electrical fire broke out.

But McKenzie was oblivious to the flames taking hold just a few feet from him. He was lost in the pain that was now flooding his body, flowing through him like blood and running into every part of his being.

As the tendrils worked their way up his neck, crawling through arteries and into his brain, he heard the pounding of great drums and saw sudden shifts of colour flash before his eyes. His hands shuddered once, then let go, and he crashed to the floor before being dragged over to the stone where the rest of the tendrils coiled about him like a snared fly in a spider web.

McKenzie was aware of none of that. His mind was lost in a void—a vision of an expanse of black, deep and unending, punctuated only by pinpricks of light. As the cosmos opened up before him he felt the pulse and throb of his heart like never before, smelt the taint of blood in the air, and heard once more that unaccountable pounding of drums. It was as though he were now moving through that unending void, past countless long-dead worlds and past indistinct shapes that moved and swam and churned in the abyssal darkness between the stars and galaxies. As the stench of blood grew stronger—so strong he could taste it now—he felt his body shrinking, diminishing within that endless night, surrounded by stars so old none had witnessed their birth. He tried to scream, but no sound escaped his lungs, and only that mocking drumming answered his silent cry as he faded into microscopic insignificance before the absolute vastness of time and space. A final scream welled up within him, a sense of great pressure building with it—like he might burst at any second. He was now so small he was less than an atom, moving unseen through a cosmos so immense and alien he couldn't even begin to comprehend it. He understood then the transient and futile nature of human endeavour, as they swarmed and struggled like insects to make a dent, a mark, on a universe so old and vast as to be untouchable, unknowable and uncaring. The span of human history amounted to nothing compared to such unending ageless expanse, and the stark realisation of the futility of all that had ever been achieved threatened to overwhelm him. He tried again to move, to make any kind of sound—but he was powerless to effect any change, spiralling down into the dark void of the abyss with the tattered edges of his sanity shredding away as he went. Desperately he tried to hold onto his mind and his thoughts, but there was so little left of him now. He was shrinking away so fast that he could feel his very consciousness unravelling even as his body broke apart…

…and then he was gone.

Back in the lab McKenzie's body was moving—shambling forward, guided by the tendrils that now emerged from the back of its head as it wrenched open cabinets and drawers, collecting scalpels, spatulas, fuses and any tools and equipment that it could lay its hands on. Already the flesh was beginning to char, the body corrupting and breaking down as a result of the energy being channelled through it.

"N'gal thul'sath Nyarrrhtep d'thuu!" it cried, forcing an alien tongue through human vocal chords as best it could as it assembled the gathered items, working as swiftly as it was able to. It discarded all but three of the items it had gathered, and carried these back over to the stone—crouching awkwardly on unfamiliar bipedal limbs to begin adjusting those nubs of crystal with the crude tools it had retrieved.

The electrical fire that had started in the corner spread rapidly now—covering the whole wall and the ceiling with searing flames, greedily consuming the piles of notes, wall-charts and furniture and spilling out into the lab next door. With nobody around to stop it, and with the doors not properly closed, there was nothing to halt its destructive progress.

McKenzie's whole body was withering away, the flesh sinking even as it blackened and peeled from the bone. Still it worked on, adjusting those exposed sections of crystal—and now a strange high pitched frequency sang out from within the heart of that device, and new sections of the pillar opened up as rods of a clear crystalline structure emerged, glowing faintly as energy coursed through them.

The collapsing form that once had been McKenzie's body shuffled around to the side of the unit. The edges of its lab coat caught alight, but still it pressed on despite the flames now running up its back, desperately trying to access some fresh nodules of crystal that were now emerging from the rear of the pillar.

It slumped awkwardly onto the floor, the head and arms burning, still struggling to twist the ends of the nodules with a scavenged pair of pliers.

A faint low rumble arose from the centre of the stone, and that fleshy heart began to pound furiously as black veins pulsed across the surface of the pillar.

A few feet in front of the device a light flared, as though being projected by those glowing crystalline rods, and the air around it rippled as if from a heat distortion.

"N'gal … th…" McKenzie's cracking throat whispered and then the blazing corpse toppled backwards, flames consuming it entirely as the pliers and equipment clattered and rolled across the floor.

The projected light swiftly widened until it formed a screen of sickly-yellow radiance in the centre of the room, less than an inch off the floor. It spread outwards, flowing over the lab benches, flaring and shifting through the visible and invisible light spectrums as it opened up, six feet across and seven feet high. From out of that strange portal a faint buzzing timbre filled the air, growing steadily in magnitude as the forming aperture took shape. With each pulse and ripple a little of the acrid smoke from within the room was sucked into the light, and a dark black fog that sunk immediately down to the floor spilled out in return.

Then something else emerged, like some obscene newborn slithering from a hellish womb—a tarry viscous mass that bubbled and seethed, oozed out with the fog, running across the floor like a mucous-coated oil-slick whose surface glistened with an iridescent sheen. It slid soundlessly across the floor, stirring up the fog, heading straight for the pillar of stone. It reached the side of the device and slid up it, forming long tube-like appendages which it now slotted into the grooves on the pillar.

In the heart of the lab the aperture of pale light shimmered once again as a gnarled crab-like append-age protruded into the room amidst another burst of heavy black fog, the reddish carapace gleaming in the firelight as the rest of it started to emerge—a mass of feelers, a seething cluster of segmented legs....

In the adjoining lab, the flames finally reached the stored oxygen and gas cylinders and licked hungrily at their sides even as the burning ceiling collapsed in around them.

The explosion, when it came, tore through al-most half the facility, blasting the windows clean out across the parking lot, and caused the upper floors to give way in a thunderous cloud of smoke, debris and flame that shook the earth and could be seen and heard for miles, and which even woke the rest of the McKenzie family from their sleep.

* * *

In the days that followed the nearby town of Eastridge got very little rest—from the job losses at the destroyed facility, to the government investigation that swooped down onto the town almost as soon as the flames were out, the safe and normal routines of daily life had been shattered for the majority of the inhabitants. For days the whole town felt numb and shocked, unwelcoming of the probing and the ques-tions by officials and wanting only to get shattered lives back on track. Most were at least grateful that the explosion had occurred so late at night—only two scientists and a security guard had been killed. But that was small comfort to their families, who looked up at that charred ruin up on the hill through grief-stricken eyes before heading home to lay one less place at the table.

But for many the losses were light, and most were thankful it hadn't been even more serious.

Thankful that is, until the first of the pets, and then shortly after children, started to go missing from back yards.

And soon after that, from within locked homes.

The Head of a Wolf

I have lost my way
I have walked this wooded path
A thousand times
And yet a wrong turn
Has found me in a place
I do not know

These trees are strange
I do not know these rocks
The ground is uneven
So this is what it is like
To be lost in recollection
To regret what one has done

I stoop by the side of the pond
Cupping my hands to drink of the water
I find them ill-suited to be my cup
They are stained, red to the elbows
And my reflection reveals not my face
But the head of a wolf

I now know my former path
Is mine no longer
These trackless wilds are mine alone
Excluded from the company of men
So must it be for the outlawed
And there is justice in my exile

— James Frederick William Rowe

Origins

Story by J Alan Erwine
Illustration by Neil T. Foster

"How long has it been?" the younger man asked his companion.

"Years," the older man mumbled without looking up.

"Do you remember what we talked about last time?"

The older man looked away, staring out the window of the orbiting café at the swirling clouds of the gas giant below them. Browns, whites, oranges, and reds danced together in organized chaos blending into new colors never before seen by the human eye, or imagined by the human mind.

"I'll take that as a yes," the younger man said with a smile, revealing his perfect white teeth.

"Take it however you like," the older man said with a grunt as he stood, "I'd just rather you take it somewhere else."

"Please, Endrick, there's no reason for hostility," the younger man said, motioning for Endrick to sit down.

Endrick sat. "How'd you find me?" he asked, staring out the window again at the stars tracing a slow path across the inky darkness of space.

"It wasn't hard. You left a virtual trace everywhere you went. It's impossible to hide when you insist on using computers."

Endrick grunted and nodded. He still wouldn't look at the younger man.

"Truth is, Endrick, you wanted me to find you."

A bellowing laugh burst forth. "You flatter yourself too much."

"Orders, please," a small waiter robot asked as it rolled up to their table.

"Nothing for me," Endrick said."

"Just an Eridanian tea for me."

"Swill."

"Me or the drink?"

Endrick smiled.

The younger man nodded. "I see you haven't lost your pathetic excuse for a sense of humor. Too bad."

The robot rolled back with his drink, which the younger man downed in one shot. "Staring at those stars and the gas giant aren't helping us solve our problem."

Endrick finally looked at the younger man. He was tall and of strong build with perfect hair and perfect complexion. The most striking feature, however, were his royal blue eyes. Obviously the young man had gone through extensive gene modification in the womb. "I wasn't aware that we had a problem, other than the fact that I was sitting here trying to enjoy the view until you came along and ruined it."

The younger man let out a short laugh and shook his head. "We could do this all day if we wanted, but I have clients waiting for me. Do you have the item?"

"And what item would that be?"

"The artifact."

Endrick nodded, stroking his unmodified profound chin slowly. "I have a number of artifacts. After all, I do sell them."

The younger man's face grew as red as the methane clouds of the gas giant below. "Come on, old man, the artifact from Tau Ceti 2. The one we talked about the last time I saw you."

Endrick looked confused. "I'm not sure I remember our previous conversation. I am getting old, after all. I'm nearly 120."

"Damn it, old man, you remember the conversation. You're just being an ass."

Several people in the café turned to glare at the two men. Loud outbursts were rare. Most of the clientele wanted to keep things quiet and private. Endrick shrugged and pointed at the younger man, who just glared back at him.

"This isn't the place for us to have this discussion."

"Oh, I think it is," Endrick said with a suddenly serious expression. "I conduct all of my business in public, and that includes with you … you little sniveling shit. I wouldn't want to be alone anywhere with you. A knife in my back or throat really isn't how I want to end my evening."

The younger man looked away to watch the glow of two ships docking a few hundred kilometers away. "Fine, we'll do this your way. Do you have the artifact or not?"

"And what artifact was that?"

"The one you excavated in the cave atop Clarke Mountain on Tau Ceti 2," the younger man whispered.

"Why do you want it?"

"I hardly think that's any of your business."

"That's what you said three and a half years ago." He looked away at a giant storm forming on the gas giant. The multi-colored, turbulent clouds were beginning to coalesce into one giant rotating mass. "Are you going to tell the people on Earth?"

The younger man shrugged.

Endrick nodded. "Fine, but the price hasn't changed."

"The money's not a problem."

Endrick motioned for a waiter robot. The robot rolled along on its wheels with an annoying squeak, drawing a glare form one or two of the customers. Sitting on its serving tray was a flat stone two feet by two feet with what looked like writing on it.

"You're sure it's a match?"

"Absolutely. It's definitely cuneiform writing matching Sumerian script."

"And its place of origin…"

"Was definitely Tau Ceti 2, dated to more than 3,500 years ago."

The younger man smiled. "Very good. I'd assume you don't want a credit transfer." He tossed a small sack onto Endrick's lap. "I think that should more than cover it."

Endrick picked up the sack and felt the gold coins jingle. "Should be more than adequate, but I have to warn you. If you tell everyone about that," he said, pointing at the stone, "It could destroy everything we think we know about ourselves."

"I'm counting on it."

First appeared in the 2001 issue of *Anotherealm*. Reprinted by permission of the author.

The Words of Mars

I didn't know the movie's Barsoomian
Would touch me so.
Their language maven went through all the books
And piled up some hundreds of the words of Mars.

No syntax, but John Carter said
It was easy to learn,
So the linguist guided his inventions
By aiming at simplicity of structure.

The result isn't a language I can understand
Watching the movie
(And it's not so good that I want to go
And see it more,
Though good enough to make me glad I went) —
But the result's a language I can recognize.

There they are, talking of tharks and jeddaks.
"Kaor!" they say in greeting.
And I haven't read the Mars books since I was a teen,
But I start to cry.

It's like recognizing your ancestral language.
Most Americans can recognize their own,
Though most can't understand them.

Barsoomian is the native language
Science fiction fans can recognize
That says they are among their landsmen.

"Kaor!" I greet the screen.

— Ruth Berman

Physics of the Stars

Story by Adam Rouse
Illustration by Morland Gonsoulin

Bzzzt

The *Star Reacher* switched to its secondary computers again. The captain cursed under his breath. According to the Agency's projections, the computers should only update every other day by this point in the journey.

"Third update in the past hour. Hold up, guys," Terrath muttered while setting his cards down. None of the three at the card table responded, already engrossed with the recalibration report.

The captain tapped at the ship-link interface on his wrist to bring up the maintenance screen onto his own contacts. Months ago, when the main computers went down the first time, Terrath worried away the seconds waiting for the all clear. The warnings became a nuisance by the fifth recalibration. With this frequency, he wondered what could be wrong with the *Star Reacher*.

Fourteen seconds passed before the variable processors in the computers came back on-line. Terrath opened the report immediately. The first screen explained why the processors had to adjust: the electrical resistance of gold in the circuits had gone down minutely. The same problem as the last seven recalibrations.

The variable processors could alter the charge they used for computations, but what were their limits? With concern, Terrath realized he didn't know. With all the recent processor resets, one of the electrical engineers should have submitted a report on this matter. A quick search showed no results. Of course not.

Terrath connected to Yerro over the ship-link and sent a mental message, *Yerro, within an hour, I want a report on how much the resistance of gold has changed since departure. Also, I want a projection on how often the processors must reset to compensate.*

A few seconds passed with only vague surly thoughts. Eventually Yerro formulated a coherent answer. *I will do as you ask, but understand, I've been watching this. In the future, please keep these demands to a minimum.*

Yerro broke off the link. The captain seethed, but decided against punishing the insolence. Theoretically, he controlled all aspects of the *Star Reacher*, but in practice, he was handcuffed until the computers or one of the science crew gave him instructions. Only another month until his turn in the deep sleep chamber and Merris would took over as captain. Then the scientists would be her problem.

With a fresh slice of humble pie churning in his stomach, Terrath continued through the screens. The third screen showed a new development. In the fifteen minutes since the last reset, the *Star Reacher* gained 0.00007 percent more mass.

Terrath gasped and almost lost his hold on the ship-link after doing the quick math. If this trend continued linearly, the *Star Reacher's* matter would mass an extra 6.5 percent by the halfway point of the journey! The highest *total* mass gain on any established star route was 4.2 percent!

Terrath tried contacting his second in command, Jimlin. However, the nav-system requested his confirmation for realigning the *Star Reacher*. Terrath banished all other concerns to oversee the course correction. A collision with a few molecules of debris knocked the ship off course by two billionth's of a degree. Even traveling an hour so far off course could send the *Star Reacher* straight into null space.

The computers made the adjustments smoothly, even with the increasing mass of the ship. Terrath checked the new heading and scratched his head. A report showed that the maneuver took more energy than expected. The extra energy was minimal to say the least, but no extra fuel consumption? Terrath couldn't see any danger, but made a note to check energy usage on future course corrections.

With the *Star Reacher's* heading adjusted, Terrath tried contacting Jimlin concerning the mass increase again. A rejected link. Jimlin alone was allowed that right as second in command and head of the science crew. Terrath resigned himself to contacting the physicist later, but hopefully the rejection meant he already noticed the changes.

Terrath minimized the ship-link from his senses only to see the three off-duty scientists still tapping at their own interfaces. Even off duty, they kept busier than him. He picked up the cards with a sigh.

Euchre was a terrible game. It was also the only game these three played on their down time. Terrath selected the jack of spades just as Goran, to his right, retrieved his own cards. The engineer looked at his hand, then the cards on the table, then back to his hand. His face scrunched dubiously and he turned to Terrath. "Captain, are you sure you don't have trump? Your card is the off-bauer this round."

Rather than ask for a refresher on the rules, Terrath laid his cards on the table. "Can we *please* play something different for once?"

Across the way, Kedda the physicist sat up straight. "You have no trump."

"Maybe," he started off coolly. "But we're either

playing something different or nothing at all today! I'll even try another one of your ancient games."

Goran looked away, but not the unflappable Kedda. "This is my favorite game. You're the only one who doesn't like it."

Silence reigned at the card table until Goran looked up at the captain with a clenched jaw and said, "Captain, respectfully, it's not just this game. You've been short with us the last few months. Today is worse. Have we upset you in some way?"

It's true. Even though the four would never be friends off the ship, Terrath shouldn't have been testy with them. "Goran, you haven't done anything. I've been on duty for almost ten years now. I'm ready to let Captain Merris take over so I can jump into the freezer."

"That only confirms you have a problem with us," Kedda pointed out.

How did the socially inept physicist catch his white lie? Goran wouldn't budge on the topic either and motioned with his hand for Terrath to continue. "Fine. If you insist… Ever since we reached cruising speed, I'm most useful as a fourth for cards.

"I can sit back and supervise, but I'm kept in the dark until the computers tell me what I have to do. It's especially frustrating right now. The computers have been recalibrating continuously … *years* away from the transition zone where we expect physics to fluctuate like this. I can't be the only one concerned by this, yet *none* of you have linked me a report as to why.

"And if you guys also do the computer's bidding, why are so many of the science crew awake? Put sixteen of you in the freezers and nobody would notice a difference. We're traveling at half the speed of light. Do you know how much easier course corrections would be if we massed thirty thousand fewer tons? Yes, that's right. For every point oh four kilos of conscious matter, we had to add a tonne of resources at departure. Yet *I'm* the one who looks expendable!"

Goran swallowed and sucked in his mild gut. "I didn't know all that. I assure you we all appreciate your efforts in running the ship."

Terrath could only shake his head at the back-handed compliment. He really shouldn't have ranted, but they pushed him into it. Marla, to his left, provided Terrath a chance to worry about something else as she tapped at her interface with increased frequency.

Marla was easily the best analyst on the *Star Reacher*. Even off duty, she'd submit a report or two for Terrath to go over. Boring material for sure, but he trusted her work second only to Jimlin.

Kedda interrupted his thoughts. "I assure you that a report will come from a human before a computer—if there is in fact a problem," she said snidely. Instead of being insulted, Terrath wondered if Marla was on that track. "We can only trust computer calculations absolutely within a couple of light years of any star."

Terrath shook his head in denial. "Kedda, when I *make* you give me a report, you find fifty different ways to tell me you've gone over the computer data and agree with the calculations. I know you guys *can* derive physical constants without the aid of the computers, but nobody is ever in the labs while on duty."

"My reports leave nothing unsaid," Kedda answered only one of Terrath's concerns. He waited for more, but she only stared at him passively.

With Kedda unrepentant as ever, Terrath backed down for Goran's sake. "For me, as long as the computers are working, they do our jobs faster and more accurately than we ever could. But when Merris takes over as captain, she *will* demand more detail in your reports."

Something Terrath said brought a smile to Goran's face. The engineer clasped his hands together and said, "Sir, in most circumstances I'd agree with your skepticism about humans being more accurate than a computer. However, the variable processors have their own limitations.

"A computer takes input-values to calculate a variable. The gravitational constant for example, right now can be anywhere between its value at the Hemate system and its unknown value around the Antries system. To solve for that variable, the computers need a gravitational force where all other factors are known. However, if the computer can't be certain that mass measurements are accurate…"

Goran obviously meant to let Terrath answer, but Kedda finished for him, "If previously known forces or measurements have become variables, the computers can only approximate a new physical constant by analyzing the error reports."

Terrath saw their point and surmised, "So with each calculation, inaccuracies in the approximation can spiral out of control?" Then logic kicked in. "No … you guys would still have problems catching a mistake in the computers. A machine that's hypothetically already askew would give you wrong numbers to work with."

"It's Malath's Intuitive Theorem," Kedda said like it made sense. "Subconsciously, sentient creatures make quick and mostly accurate approximations in relation to the current physical reality."

Goran stepped in to supply an example. "If I were to crumple up a piece of paper and toss it once—when I haven't yet experienced the current physics—I'll intuitively understand how far a second toss should go. Regardless of what I experienced, a computer will calculate only according to the possibly incorrect data it received. If I *think* the paper will go four meters, but the computer tells me it'll go twelve, I know the computer is wrong without even needing to make the second toss."

Goran finished with a flourish of his hands, but Terrath had to keep a groan from escaping. "I followed your example. However, that means you guys should be using the experimentation equipment the entire time you're on duty!"

Goran prevented Kedda from responding with a hand on her arm and a shake of his head. The engineer screwed his eyes up as if racking his brain for a long lost name or detail. Terrath waited patiently since listening to Goran's lecture kept his mind off of Marla's unknown project.

Finally, Goran looked down with a smile. "Okay. You know that the star, Caurous, is off limits. Right?"

Terrath nodded. Caurous and five other stars carried the designation of being 'dead zones.' "Is that the star where water is an ineffective solvent?" Terrath asked.

"Yes. The physical constants around Caurous call for less electron affinity of many elements, but most importantly, oxygen. However, the star system is overwhelmingly hydrogen and helium. That's all the computers had to work with. It took a human physicist to use the data gathered from observing hydrogen and helium to extrapolate it to other elements."

Kedda gave her rendition of this history lesson. "Lower electron affinity for oxygen reduces the dipole strength of water molecules. The ions dissolved in our bodies would crystallize and kill us."

Goran nodded her direction and finished, "You see, Captain, our job is more than knowing and deriving the laws as they shift. We can detect faulty or incomplete calculations. The experimentation equipment is only useful for quickly catching a flaw in the computers while we're in the transition zone."

Terrath swallowed his frustration and asked, "So when you three are on duty, you're essentially proofing the computer's work, not just scanning it?" Goran bobbed his head enthusiastically. Terrath

licked his lips and looked over to the still-busy Marla. "In that case, what trends in constant-fluctuation are affecting us most so far?"

Kedda answered with cold efficiency. "Most importantly, a large increase to the gravitational constant. Though matter shall remain stable because of fluctuations that govern the strong force and electromagnetism." Goran used his fingers to tick off her points then added his agreement.

After the terrible story of Caurous, Marla's lack of an answer bothered Terrath more than their lack of worry. "Have you two considered that the ship's mass is increasing? Will there be a problem as we fully experience the physics of Antries?"

"Gravity and mass issues are Jimlin's responsibility," Kedda deflected.

Bzzzt

Terrath gave up on grilling the two and all three accessed their ship-link interfaces. The recalibration of the variable processors only took a few seconds to Terrath's mild surprise. The indicators he usually checked were in the green, but he took his time, paying more attention to the raw data.

"Captain!" the single word didn't come through the ship-link.

Terrath hid the screens and saw Marla staring at him wide eyed and quivering. "Yes, Marla?" Terrath asked, already fearing the worst.

"Captain, you have to turn us around. We can't continue forward!"

Springing to his mind were a dozen disaster situations. In the simulators, he passed every scenario—except for the nova test—with over eighty percent of the crew surviving. Stopping a vessel moving at half the speed of light was never the correct response.

Terrath blocked out his initial fear. He'd know what to do after understanding the problem. Before responding, Terrath stood up from the table to establish authority. Marla stood as well, but leaned against her chair still shaking. Keeping his voice even, Terrath ordered, "Marla, calm yourself. I need details."

Slower, but with stress creasing every word, Marla reiterated, "Captain, if we don't turn around now, you put everyone's life at risk. There's an anomalous star somewhere on this route. The ship will likely cease to function if we continue forward."

An anomalous star?! There were no simulations in his training on anomalous stars. How could there be when it's impossible to know what problems they would pose? Or what they're even made of?! There were always the basics of ship and crew preservation to fall back on, but first…

Terrath forced an emergency connection to his second in command. *Jimlin, there's a possible anomalous star. Put the entire science crew on duty. Assign them as you see fit. We need to know everything we can about this star ASAP.*

Sh… Jimlin only let half of the thought-out curse get through to Terrath. *I started to suspect it myself when my models began drifting. Glad someone caught it before me. Who would that be?*

Marla. Now get to the rest!

A few seconds of silence passed before Jimlin returned with, *I already had, sir. I needed Marla's work so I can go over it myself. I have that now as well. We'll meet in person when I know more.*

Dumbstruck, Terrath was essentially being ordered to wait patiently in a time of crisis. Only someone with a captain's training could possibly know how to avoid an anomalous star. If the situation weren't so dire, he'd demote Jimlin on the spot for such gross insolence. As it stood, he couldn't take the first step until he knew everything that the science crew did. Terrath was forced to respond, *I'll be waiting at the bridge. Let me know as soon as possible if there's something we can do.*

Terrath let the ship-link conversation drop and started to ask Marla to continue, but she and the other two were already out of the break room and it sounded like they were jogging toward the computer labs.

Terrath refused to indulge in spiteful thoughts about Jimlin having more real authority. There was still much he could do before the science crew linked him a report on the anomalous star. First, he needed someone with a more tactical and prudent mind on his side.

He activated the ship-link again and input the override codes to begin Captain Merris' wake up. He had to confirm three times before the chamber began the thawing process earlier than scheduled. The program predicted she would regain basic consciousness in thirteen hours, so Terrath scheduled an urgent reminder in eleven.

While working with the sleep programs, Terrath must have unconsciously wandered the rotating corridor past dormitories, labs and hygiene facilities. In front of him were the sealed double doors of the bridge, waiting stoically for a captain.

Terrath swallowed, then stepped up to manually input his code. The security doors slid open silently. He stepped over the threshold to a quiet hum as the control room awakened from years of stand-by. He took in the thousands of buttons, switches and knobs. He hadn't touched a single one of them since departure from Hemate, but still knew the function of each one. That knowledge might be put to the test depending on what was in store for the *Star Reacher.*

The doors shifted closed automatically, leaving Terrath alone with his thoughts. He started a diagnostic check on all the control boards and turned around in the small space behind the captain's chair. From this room, virtually every function on the ship could be overridden. At high speeds, it was essentially forbidden to touch anything. That was unless the ship was damaged, a mutiny was in process or … when an anomalous star made it necessary.

Captain, I'm outside the bridge. May I come in? Terrath shook in surprise at Jimlin's request through the ship-link. How long was he lost in thought?

I'll have the doors open in a second. Terrath keyed in the codes to deactivate the control panels and then opened up the bridge. The doors split open to reveal not just Jimlin, but Marla too. The two scientists squeezed into the room, standing almost chest to chest before the doors had clearance to close again.

Terrath clenched his teeth to avoid saying he never invited Marla to join the two. Jimlin implied he would have already gone through Marla's report. She should be working with the others.

"Sir, I did as you asked," Jimlin said, almost as if Terrath's consternation was audible. "Marla is here to explain what she knows of HAAS—that's the name we're using for the Hemate-Antries Anomalous Star."

They named the star without talking to him? No, that didn't really matter. "Fine. Marla, make it quick," Terrath replied, terse and quick.

Terrath ground his teeth when the analyst stepped back and bumped into a bank of—thankfully—deactivated control panels. "Sir, it's still conjecture, but I believe we're dealing with an event that's similar to an inactive dwarf star. With no movement through magnetic mechanisms…"

That told Terrath nothing. "Get to the point!" he interrupted.

Marla blinked rapidly several times before continuing. "Uh, near HAAS, my calculations show that physical constants affecting the radii of charged particles in a magnetic field will create a result always approaching zero. If we get too close to this anomalous star, electric motors won't work… No matter how much juice we drop into them."

Terrath expected to hear about the alarming mass increase. Not a new problem. "You're saying that if we get too close, we'll have to switch propulsion over to manual?" Marla and Jimlin each raised their eyebrows. Of course they wouldn't know about the option of disengaging propulsion from the motors. It was an emergency feature for slow in-system travel in case a nova fried the computer systems. The one simulation he couldn't pass in training...

"...at half the speed of light?" was all Jimlin had to say in rebuttal. The two stared at each other in silence. The only noise was from Marla as she started to tap at her ship-link interface.

Terrath shook his head, "No, Jimlin, it's not designed for use at cruising speed. But if the computers won't work, what other choice do we have?"

"Like Marla told you, we turn around. Captain, HAAS will doom the *Star Reacher*. Everything on-board is controlled electronically. Even if the engines can be disconnected from the computers, it's not a simple issue of piloting us past HAAS."

Terrath took a long slow breath. "Jimlin, I need to be informed about everything in front of us. Stopping is not as easy as you suggest. Now please, tell me about this HAAS of yours so I can make an informed decision."

Jimlin squeezed his lips together and took an equally long and audible breath through his nose. "Captain, honestly you're not educated enough to decide what we should do in relation to HAAS."

Terrath's vision dimmed and he swore he heard an audible snap as his last shred of patience broke like a twig. "I am the captain of this ship, damn it! If I tell the computers to cut off oxygen supply, it will! Oh, you object to that because it'll kill us all? You know what? If I blindly do what you say, we'll be just as dead!"

Jimlin had already backed up against the doors and Terrath ended his tirade almost nose to nose with the man. He stepped back to the chair, giving the second in command room to wipe his face. Marla was unfazed through it all, still tapping at her wrist.

Terrath grimaced, realizing how childish his outburst sounded. This wasn't the time to apologize or back down though. He needed to regain control. "Look, we both need input from each other. I don't know what lies in store with HAAS as we get closer and you don't know the limits of a ship this size. We *have* to work together."

Jimlin's throat bobbed as he swallowed hard. "Sir, I apologize for being out of line. You're right.

We need to combine our efforts toward getting back to Hemate."

His response wasn't good enough, so Terrath simply ordered, "Piggy-back onto my profile and I'll show you the resource problems we'll encounter turning back."

With Jimlin able to see the same screens as Terrath, the captain ran through calculations to show: a stopping time between fourteen and nineteen months—depending on the mass increase which also raised *Star Reacher's* momentum; a maximum safe return speed of one eighth the speed of light; travel duration of at least forty years—much worse than the twenty five years Terrath guessed at with mental math; finally an estimation of over half the crew perishing due to resource shortages.

Terrath dropped the ship-link from their senses. "What I showed you doesn't *touch* on the difficulty of stopping in a vacuum. When ejecting matter forward, we'll invariably collide with at least some of it. Each collision alters our course. With no computer assistance, how can we avoid drifting into null space?"

Jimlin looked away, but Terrath couldn't tell if it was frustration at not being listened too, or if the man felt ashamed. When Jimlin finally spoke, his flat emotionless tone didn't give Terrath any insight. "Well, we still can't go forward."

"I do trust you on that. There are other options though. We can perform an unpowered slingshot around HAAS and leave on a corridor between two other stars. However, that will require the absolute position of HAAS. We also need to know the exact kinetic physics. Do we know either of those things yet?"

Jimlin shook his head minutely. "Though, I predict we'll know the location in a week or two. As an anomalous star, the matter of HAAS either doesn't exist in a traditional sense, or it has no emissions we can pick up on our scanners. We have to compare test results as we continue along."

"Do we know anything about the physics of HAAS? Other than that electricity is a moot issue? If we get too close will our nerves still function?" Terrath prodded.

"Captain, we're working on that as well. I'm not big on the biology side of things, but I understand that our nerves work via direct ion interaction. Life should be technically possible." Jimlin looked down at his feet. "Though I do see how I have been hasty and made your job difficult. I thought we had to at least take a chance at returning to Hemate."

"Jimlin," Terrath paused. He was tired of always

acting contrite when a scientist undermined his authority. He still needed to do it this time. "I'm truly sorry I flew off the handle. All that's important is that we find a way to survive this disaster."

The physicist wiped his brow again and then responded in his familiar exacting tone, "May I suggest slowing down while we still have computer assistance? It'll give us more time to find the answers you need, Captain."

Terrath compared the pros and cons of slowing down the *Star Reacher*. Then to Jimlin he said, "There are certain options that would benefit from more speed. First, we need to know a few basics about the kinetic physics. I want to inform everyone about HAAS and then you can set the science crew to their tasks."

"I'll have the group-link set up in a few seconds, Captain." Jimlin's eyes glazed over and he started to tap at his wrist efficiently.

With Jimlin at work, Terrath pulled up the computer report concerning the last course correction. Marla said that electric motors wouldn't work no matter how much power they had. If that was true and the sudden increase in mass was also because of HAAS, it might explain the earlier problem with the nav system.

Terrath broke down the report so it showed him the course correction step by step. The computers predicted fuel use perfectly, but had a difficult time aligning the engines before the burn. The nozzles had to be re-shaped just minutely, but three times refused to move with the nano-pulse of energy. The problem Marla found was already present.

I have the group link ready for you to join, sir, Jimlin's message came through the ship-link.

Terrath tried burying his recent discovery into the back of his mind and then joined the group-link. Dozens of profiles were seemingly half on his mental periphery and half beyond perception. Even without the intimacy of a single link, if he wavered, they would all know it.

Some of you have already heard that there is an anomalous star in our path. He waited as the inevitable wave of shock and fear became half thoughts from the maintenance and service crew members. *We have caught it early and with hard work will find a way to continue on.*

Terrath instantly regretted his choice of words as an uproar of questions assaulted him. There were many variants, but each question boiled down to, *Why are we not turning back?*

He had to mute the input from everyone else and explained. *Stopping the* Star Reacher *will take at least fourteen months. Already, we're losing some control of the engines because of this anomalous star. We will surely drift into null space with no control of our trajectory if I begin the reversal now.* He took the mute off and added, *Jimlin will now explain what we're dealing with and what we need to do as a crew to pull through.*

No direct words were formulated by the crowd, but Jimlin contended with a storm of confused half thoughts. *We are learning more even as we speak. I just recently had confirmation that HAAS—the name for this anomalous star—is classified as a black hole.*

Terrath couldn't let the crew sense his chagrin; they were upset enough. Marla tried to describe HAAS, but he had cut her off. If he'd listened, the black hole verdict wouldn't have been a surprise.

When the mental tumult calmed down enough, Jimlin continued, *We're basing this conclusion on mass, gravity and an absence of certain energy emissions. We won't have to worry about traditional threats associated with black holes though. If there were a chance for us to pass into the event horizon, our view of Antries from Hemate would have been distorted. The real problem we're faced with is a loss of electrical control of the ship. This will be in effect once we're experiencing the full influence of HAAS.*

Another storm of thoughts and questions followed. Terrath had to mute them again and declare, *We can't avoid HAAS completely with our current speed, but as we learn more, other options of surviving may become available.*

Then, he ordered, *From all the non-science crew, I need a step up in service. The science crew will be awake many hours at a time. Those who are capable of simple information collation, I want you available to take over simple tasks currently done by the science crew. Of you on the science crew, I want you following Jimlin's orders, but please keep me continually updated on the expected kinetic physics of HAAS from a radius of two to four light years. It will be critical to know the exact forces working on the* Star Reacher *for a possible pre-programmed flight path around it.*

Terrath un-muted the group to allow Jimlin to say more, but anger burst forth over the ship-link. Of all the jumbled thoughts, one very clear question came through from an air-systems mechanic. *How can you consider anything but turning around? It sounds like we still have light years to turn back. You can't throw our lives away like this!*

Terrath was ready to silence them and explain, but Jimlin answered the man with clear vitriolic words, *The captain has decided it's impossible to turn around. He would never suggest going forward unless it was in our best interest.*

Stunned silence. The only response was from Marla—not using the group-link, but to him directly. *Captain! I had an idea about electricity. I've had the computer check my work a dozen times and electricity* should *flow through circuits even on the surface of HAAS. It just won't result in any kinetic force. So we won't be able to produce energy with the reactor, but batteries will work. Still, that means the computers can function with just a few tweaks!*

At first, Terrath was frustrated Marla wasn't paying attention during the meeting. It didn't matter if the computers would still work if they couldn't control navigation, the waste re-formulators, or the life support pumps in the deep sleep chambers. Going over what she said a second time though, an idea still unformed started to percolate.

Marla, please tell me that our only problems near HAAS will be the increased gravity, increased mass and no motion through electric or magnetic fields.

Um, I think that's what I'm saying. All other factors seem to be within the range of what the Star Reacher *can handle. Others will have to check my work on biological conditions. I was more focused on…*

Terrath missed the last of her words as he lost control of the link and slid back to the bridge and his normal five senses. He edged around the oblivious forms of Jimlin and Marla to collapse in the captain's chair. A thick pane of translucent metal showed the stars ahead. One of them was Hemate. Unable to be seen was HAAS. Somewhere also unseen was the immediate future and possible eternal recognition and glory.

Did Marla understand the implications of suggesting that HAAS might be a highly survivable black hole? For centuries the Agency and all mankind had been searching for the theoretical gateway to other galaxies. A celestial engine able to charge matter with enough kinetic energy to surpass the normal constraints of space and time.

"Captain. Captain, are you okay?" Jimlin asked while shaking Terrath's shoulder. Terrath rotated in the chair and nodded with a smile. "You left the group link suddenly. Then Marla told me you dropped a link with her too. What's wrong?"

"Jimlin, what if I were to suggest that HAAS might be a survivable black hole like the one that scientists have theorized about for hundreds of years?"

Jimlin's eyes and mouth gaped open together. "I … I'd find it unlikely we stumbled upon one. But then I'd say we have to find out!" The physicist shook his head. "No … Marla told me about her revelation and I agree HAAS isn't as deadly as we first thought. Still, we won't have control of the *Star Reacher*. The forces might not kill us, but secondary problems still can."

Terrath took the caution almost on deaf ears while reliving the days of his youth. In particular, the day he joined the Agency with a dream that he would be the captain to discover a star truly unique. Years of training, more years of boredom and acting as a computer's gofer turned Terrath into the resource manager he feared becoming. He had forgotten his dreams, but here they were again. This time a reality.

"Captain, are you listening?" Jimlin interrupted Terrath's fantasy again. "Personally, I would love to see if you're right about HAAS. Even if it means we don't make it. However, we have the crew to protect. We have to trust that those who follow us will be better prepared to deal with the unique physics." Jimlin still cautioned Terrath, but this time his words lacked the firm conviction ever-present in the man's voice for the past ten years.

"Jimlin, if you're willing to risk your life to see if HAAS can open up other galaxies to us, why wouldn't the rest of the crew do the same?" The physicist's eyes popped open in shock and he leaned back against the closed door. He eventually nodded slowly and Terrath went on, "Every one of us signed on for this mission aware of the danger. Aware that dozens of ships were lost on charting missions before us."

Jimlin bit his bottom lip as he looked past Terrath toward the translucent pane. "You're right, but you make it sound like we all boarded the *Star Reacher* expecting to die out here."

"Not at all. We just know that avoiding danger doesn't mean we'll stay alive…"

"Just that we avoided living to our fullest," Jimlin finished Terrath's point with his own words. The scientist locked eyes with Terrath and declared, "Especially when something so great is possibly within our grasp. Captain, I support your decision. Do you already have plans on how we'll survive with no electric control of the ship?"

Bzzzt the computers warned, but neither man paid it any heed.

Terrath smiled. A few minutes ago, Jimlin—most likely every scientist—wouldn't trust his decision unless they suggested it first. "I do have some ideas. We'll wake the entire crew, train them on the manual controls and ration our battery charge for as long as the reactor will be useless."

Jimlin whistled. "That's a lot of variables. Do you think it'll work?"

With real excitement for the first time in years, Terrath answered, "There's only one way to know for certain!"

Through Fire Across Ether

Air. Water. Land.
The elements.
Earth and sky.

Stars. Galaxies. Clusters.
Einstein-Rosen bridges.
Dying worlds and just born ones.

Before. Now. After.
Eons.
In and out of space and time.

We belong here and there.
We belong anywhere.
We belong nowhere.

This one reality.
That other one.
Some again and countless more.

Everything and its contrary.
Nothing and its equal.
They all are and they all are not.

We come and we go.
Far beyond where we think we may.
So far away and yet ever as close.

— Alessio Zanelli

Circe

The lost sailor
From a distant land
Drawing close
To the unknown
Harbour
Of her eyes

The open balcony
The distant sound
Of traffic
On the boulevard
Like hidden waves
On a midnight shore

Tapers are burning
All around her bed
The pale smoke
Rising to the paper
Chinese lanterns
Stirring gently
In the summer air

And then
The capture
Of the kiss
The serpent's hiss
Of silk on skin
The crackling static
Of her black hair
The end
Of care

— William Corner Clarke

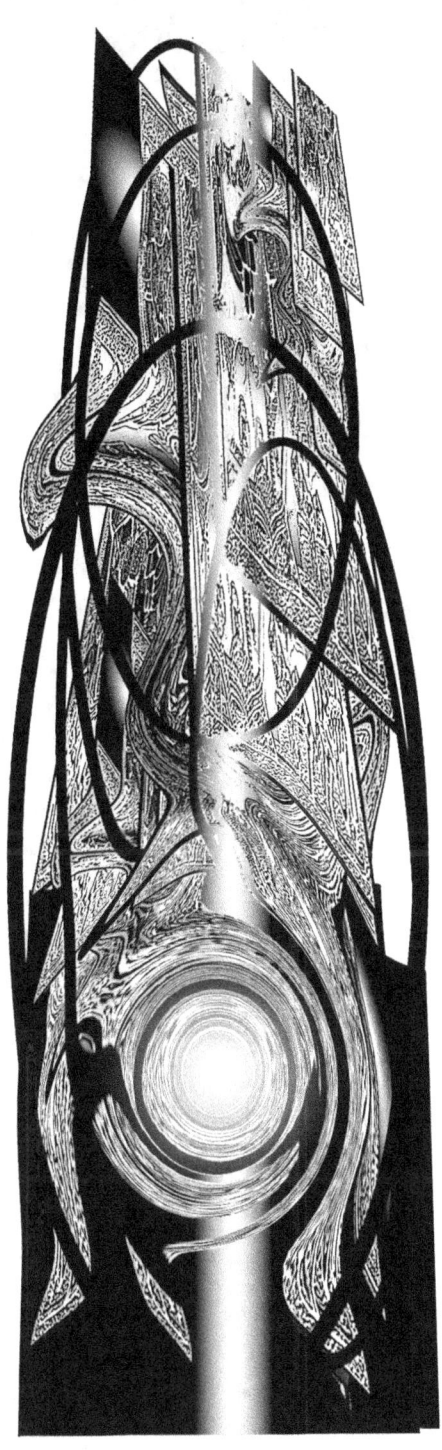

The Empty Road

The road lies ahead,
Brown and bare,
Turning the pallid sky
Gray like a shroud.

I am holding their hands,
Small as birds, unlined
With promise, while mine,
Marked with crisscrossed crevices

Are deep as trenches
Within my parchment skin.
Our species' sign of maturity;
A time to take flight.

As the day sighs and sleeps,
The sun falls quickly
Like a shooting star,
One we wish upon every night

When we pray for transcendence
And wisdom to lead our young.
Bright eyes turn to look at me.
I nod. We are almost there.

The moon peers out from our horizon.
She does not dare loom too large
As the deep black night unfurls
Across the planet, extinguishing

Every fragment of light.

We stand proud before the darkness,
Cast aside the shroud hiding us,
Stretch out the wings
That were our birthright

And fly into the night.

— Christina Sng

Io

Story by Jeremy Terry
Illustration by Teresa Tunaley

People have said a person doesn't dream in cryosleep, that it is like blinking. One second you're awake then you blink and you're in a different time and place when you open your eyes.

It was not so with Register.

Register dreamed. He dreamed of days gone by, of childhood fantasies, lurid sexual trysts, and horrors. He dreamed of his father and the way he always smelled of the pipe tobacco he smoked when he was working in the shed behind their home. He dreamed of his mother and the crystalline sound of her voice raised in chorus with the congregation of the First Baptist Church where he attended in his youth.

Mostly, he dreamed about Katy.

They met in college, he the party animal, she an angel of integrity. It was love at first sight the day he saw her across campus walking with a group of friends. Her brunette hair blew in the autumn breeze, catching the sun's golden rays. She was perfect. He began walking her direction but halted when an odd ringing sounded. He looked towards the university's chapel and saw a man waving to him. Register thought him a stranger until the man called his name. The ringing repeated, sounding like the world's biggest alarm clock, hastening recollection. He did know the man, but he wasn't supposed to be there. He came much later, after the accident, after Katy…

No, he thought, turning away from the man. She was *there*. She was *safe*. All he need do was cross the grass and take her in his arms and then everything would be all right with the world. Everything—

"Wake up, Register! God damn it, wake your sorry ass up!"

Register shook his head in childlike defiance. He was where he belonged and he wouldn't let anyone take him away from her. He ran towards Katy with outstretched hands, calling her name, but something was wrong. The sunlight was getting brighter. It grew harsh and sterile and it gave no warmth. He could see nothing but the white light.

"Wake up…"

* * *

Register likened waking from cryosleep to being born or at least what he imagined being born to be like, rising up from wet darkness into stark light. It was a truly traumatic experience.

"Breathe!" shouted Medical Officer O'Halleran, "You'll be all right!"

Register gagged, vomiting thick strings of the inorganic jelly used to suspend a body during stasis to protect it from the crushing g-forces generated by a starship's engines. It was completely harmless but it tasted like shit. Swallowing some was inevitable during the waking process.

O'Halleran patted him on the back, "There you go. Are you feeling better now?"

Register coughed up more slime, "I hate this job."

The medic laughed and walked away to help Rogers, the ship's engineer and mechanic. Register glanced around as the rest of the U.N.S. *Hope's* crew began to stir. First Officer Maitlin, a stern looking middle aged woman with salt and pepper hair, stood talking with Analiese, the only other woman on board and the ship's pilot. Both women wore only their government issued faded green undergarments. If they minded his perusal they gave no indication. Captain Burke stood behind them sipping his steaming coffee and watching his crew with a satisfied expression on his chiseled face.

"All right people," Burke said. "Let's get to it. Get yourselves washed up. I expect everyone on the bridge in fifteen."

"Aye, sir," said Maitlin. "You heard the captain, folks. Hop to it."

Register fell in line behind Rogers and O'Halleran as they exited the cryobay into a small locker room and shower area. He stripped off his boxers and stepped under a showerhead, letting the hot water cascade down his muscular frame, washing the jelly from his body. He sighed, feeling like a human being again. He heard laughter in the stall beside him and glanced over to see Rogers leaning over the next wall staring at Analiese.

"Damn," he said, shaking his head, "I'd love to bite that ass, baby."

Analiese rolled her eyes, "You can't handle this."

"He can't even handle himself without a pair of tweezers and a magnifying glass," called Maitlin from her shower across the room.

"Ouch," laughed O'Halleran. "First got you there man."

"It's cold in here," grumbled Rogers as he turned back to the water. "Things shrink when it's cold…"

Register turned off the water and toweled off, tuning the others banter out. His dreams of Katy had put him in a melancholy mood and he had no interest in their games. He dressed quietly and walked out into the companionway.

The United Nations Starship *Hope* was designed

in much the same style as Aircraft Carriers and Destroyers from the twentieth and twenty-first centuries, built to make the most use of the interior space with little concern for comfort. Register descended two levels, crossed over amidships, and climbed up three levels to the bridge where Captain Burke was waiting. They were joined five minutes later by the rest of the crew.

"Okay," Burke said, "I'm sure you're all curious about our little trip. I apologize for the secrecy but orders came down from way above my pay grade to hold off on briefing you until we arrived at our destination."

"What is our destination?" asked O'Halleran.

"We're currently in orbit above Saturn."

Register felt a wave of excitement rush through him and he smiled. He was no rookie but this was the first time he'd been on mission this deep in space. It was the chance of a lifetime to see Saturn up close with his own eyes.

"United Nations Command received a distress signal originating from Titan, Saturn's largest moon. It's been confirmed that the beacon belongs to a deep space research team Command dispatched some eleven months ago. Our job it to locate the team and rescue any survivors. Are there any questions?"

Analiese raised her hand. "What kind of research were they conducting?"

"That's classified. We don't need to know what they were doing. All we need to know is Saturn-space is a long way from home and extremely dangerous. One mistake out here and one or maybe all of us won't get to go home."

Rogers licked his lips, "I got a hot little number waiting for me back on Earth so you wankers better bring your "A" game."

Maitlin rolled her eyes. "You're vile, Rogers."

"I love you too, pumpkin."

"Enough," said Burke. He looked around. "Are there any more intelligent questions?"

No one spoke up.

"Good, then everyone get to your stations and let's get this over with."

The crew dispersed to various consoles around the bridge, the captain and Maitlin center stage, Analiese at the front. She keyed commands into her computer and the blast shield covering the bridge's viewport retracted revealing a sight beyond description. For a moment they were all struck silent. Saturn's gaseous atmosphere swirled and shifted like an amber sea, its rings shining like gold. A dark mass floated between them and the planet, slowly drifting towards them.

"That's Titan," said Burke. "First, do you have grid coordinates on the beacon?"

"Aye, sir, the signal's coming from the moon's dark side. I'm sending the coordinates to Analiese now."

"Coordinates received," Analiese said.

"Take us down to the surface," ordered Burke.

Register watched from his post beside Rogers as the U.N.S. *Hope* descended towards the desolate satellite. Rogers's screens displayed ever changing readouts and telemetry from around the ship, everything from minute changes in temperature and pressure on the hull to the status of the ship's mechanical and electrical systems. Register looked to his own screen which was scrolling through data concerning the moon. Titan's surface was showing a temperature of almost -260 degrees Fahrenheit.

"Captain," he called. "I'm seeing extreme cold on the ground. We won't be able to handle the conditions down there for long, sir."

"Duly noted, Mr. Register. You heard him, people. We go in, we get out. No fucking around."

A chorus of "aye, sir" went up about the bridge. Outside the viewing port the moon's midnight surface loomed like the black seas of Hell. Looking down on the dark expanse gave Register an odd sensation of vertigo. He turned his eyes back to his monitor.

"Sir," Maitlin said, "I'm picking up a high level of radiation near the beacon. Their ship's reactor may have gone into meltdown."

"Is the level too great for our suits' shielding, Mr. Register?"

Maitlin sent the information to Register's screen. He studied the jagged green spikes on the graph for a moment and then addressed the captain. "The shielding is sufficient. Again, it's a matter of timing. Prolonged exposure to the cold will be just as fatal as the radiation."

"Roger that."

Register risked another glance out the viewing port in time to see the last sliver of Saturn vanishing beyond the horizon. A minute passed in silence as Analiese worked at the pilot's console. "We're nearing the coordinates, Captain."

"Bring up the external lights Mr. Rogers."

Rogers keyed in a command and several screens attached to the bulkhead above Analiese flickered to life showing feeds from close circuit cameras attached to the *Hope's* hull. The moon's surface was rocky and desolate. One monitor showed a glossy vein of obsidian, evidence of a volcanic eruption from ages past. Register found the melancholy landscape beautiful. He thought about what it would be like to be castaway in such a barren place, cold and forever silent. It was a place he could find peace, a place he could be alone with his memories of Katy.

"Sir," called Maitlin. "The beacon is at the base of the small mountain on our port side."

"Circle the area and then set us down a hundred meters from the site."

Analiese brought the *Hope* around, bringing the powerful floodlights to bear on their objective.

"Jesus wept…" whispered the pilot.

The research team's vessel lay scattered in pieces along a mile long trough dug into the moon's surface. The largest section was partially buried in an avalanche caused by the crash, the ship's nose and bridge entombed in the mountainside.

"That explains the radiation signature," Rogers said. "A crash like that would crack the ship's reactor like an egg."

"How did anyone survive to activate the beacon?" O'Halleran asked.

Analiese finished her circuit of the wreckage and began to direct the spacecraft along the trough, looking for a suitable landing spot.

"Wait," called Burke. "Come back around and hover over the skid twenty meters from the crash. I thought I saw something… There it is! Rogers, zoom in."

"What is that?" asked Register.

"It's our missing researchers, or at least some of them."

They were there on Titan's surface, four white shapes around a fifth figure. Register's heart sank at the sight. The *Hope's* mission had just shifted from rescue to body recovery.

"Is there any chance they may still be alive?" Analiese aske.

"None," Register replied quietly.

Captain Burke sighed. "Set us down Analiese. Let's get this over with so we can go home."

The pilot landed the *Hope* on the rocky surface, the starship's inertial dampeners cushioning the craft so its crew didn't even notice when it touched down.

Burke stood. "All right, Register, O'Halleran, and I will be the retrieval team. First, you have the bridge."

Maitlin nodded. "Aye, Captain. You three be careful out there."

* * *

Register slinked around the tiny airlock compartment checking to make sure the captain and O'Halleran's suits were donned properly. There was zero room for error. One minute crack in a seal would spell death. Satisfied with what he found, Register turned and depressed the button to begin purging the airlock. The process took mere seconds and then the outer hatch was sliding open and Titan's chill embraced them.

Static crackled in Register's helmet and then Maitlin's voice came through. "All right, the researchers are thirty meters straight ahead. You can't miss them."

"Copy that," said Burke. "We're exiting the airlock now."

The three men stepped out onto the moon's surface and started forward, their bouncing tread ungainly in the low gravity. Register stared around in awe. The trough's walls rose above them twenty feet on each side and its track ran out before them into complete darkness. The scale of it all made him feel very small. He looked ahead and saw something odd. The researchers lay at the dim edge of the *Hope's* floodlights and yet the area around them was bright as day as though the scientists themselves gave off a bluish light.

O'Halleran turned to the others. "Are you seeing this?"

"What do you think is causing it?" asked Burke. "Radiation from their ship?"

Register shook his head. "This isn't like any radiation I've ever seen. It reminds me more of bioluminescence observed in deep sea life on Earth."

"Whatever it is, I don't like it. Captain Burke to *Hope*, do you copy?"

"Go ahead, Captain."

"First, I want you to prepare five portable cryopods and place them in the airlock. There's something hinky with these bodies and I want them quarantined until we can figure out what's going on with them."

"Aye, sir, I'll have them ready."

"Good, thank you. Mr. O'Halleran if it's biolum … uh … what Register said wouldn't this be your area of expertise? What could cause this in a human?"

"I'm no biologist but I know bioluminescence is caused by bacteria. I'll do a culture once we have the bodies on the *Hope*. Maybe I'll get lucky and figure it out."

"Just do your best. I can't ask for more than…" He trailed off into silence and the three men stopped and stared.

They'd reached the researchers.

Four of them lay on the ground around a central figure, their suits torn, their helmets removed. They stared with frozen eyes, rapture in their gaze. Register looked where they looked and worshipped with them. The woman was nude. Her pale skin shone with a blue glow, her raven hair fell about her firm breasts and pink nipples. She was perfect. Like Io, the mortal woman who captured the heart of Zeus himself, she captured his heart.

Katy, he thought. *She looks like Katy.*

"What the fuck is this?" asked O'Halleran.

"Beautiful," whispered Register.

"What was that, Mr. Register?"

"Uh … nothing…"

"Why would they take their helmets off? Where'd the girl come from? I don't like this, Captain. Something isn't right here."

"Maybe," Burke said, "but what do you suggest we do about it? Should we leave the bodies and go home?"

The thought of leaving the woman behind terrified Register beyond description. Having seen her he couldn't fathom being parted from her ever again.

"Well, no sir," O'Halleran responded, "but—"

"No 'buts,'" said Burke. "Our mission stands. We retrieve the bodies and we take them home to their families."

"Aye sir."

The captain turned to Register. "Go back to the *Hope* and get five anti-grav suspension units. We'll use them to transport the bodies to the ship. No one touches them until we know what happened to them out here."

"Y-yes, sir," replied Register. He took one more look at the woman, the goddess, and then set off for the *Hope*.

* * *

Alone at last, thought Register as he emerged from the shadowy alcove across the hall from the cryobay. He'd been quietly biding his time since the goddess was brought on board. Now they were underway, thousands of miles from Saturn and its moons, and the rest of the crew were preparing to put the *Hope* on autopilot so they could climb into their cryotubes for the trip home. He walked through the door into the locker room, laughing at how nervous he was. He felt like he was in high school again, about to pick up a girl for his first date. He exited into the cryobay and paused, staring across the dimly lit room

at the five portable pods nestled against the wall, each exuding a soft blue radiance.

Register crossed the room to the last pod. She was there in all her glory, more gorgeous than a spring morning. He longed to touch her, to kiss her lips, her neck, her breasts. If only—

She opened her eyes.

They were black like her hair and deep as the sea. They caught the overhead lights and reflected them back in a million white points. Looking into them was like looking at a starry night sky.

"Help me," she begged, though her full lips never moved. Her voice was in his mind, speaking to him with a voice so familiar it brought tears to his eyes.

"Katy?"

"Help me, Reggie. I'm so cold in this box. Please, let me out."

"This isn't possible… You died years ago…"

The woman squirmed erotically, rubbing her slender hands down her abdomen and into her dark pubic mound, "Help me, Reggie. I want you so bad… Touch me… Love me… Release me and we can be together forever."

Register knew something was wrong. He felt it deep down in the animalistic recesses of his subconscious, the part of him which still lived by ancient instinct and primal fear, but he was powerless against her gaze and voice. He watched as his hands reached for the pod's keypad and began entering the unlock code.

"Yes, Reggie, that's it!" She smiled, revealing teeth the color of blood and sharp as razors.

He might have fled then if not for the smell of roses that came floating to him as the cryopod opened. Katy wore perfume that smelled like that.

"Oh, Katy," he moaned, reaching out to take her in his arms. He touched her flesh and screamed. It was like ice and hard as stone. He pulled his hand back, seeing her as she truly was for the first time. The illusion was torn away, the horror laid bare. The thing before Register was virtually faceless, the only features cavernous holes where its eyes should be and its blood-red, teeth-filled maw. Its sexless body pulsed with an unhealthy light, not blue but a poisonous green-yellow.

"Be mine," it said in Katy's voice, the only part of the lie it still held onto. "Be with me forever… Love me forever…"

Register screamed again and ran, sure each step would be his last, sure he would feel the monster's frozen hands at his throat. He gained the hall and fled up the path, chased by echoes and nightmares. He crossed amidships and went up, seeking safety in numbers on the bridge with the rest of the crew.

"My God, man!" exclaimed Maitlin as he burst in, tripping over his own feet and sprawling on the floor. "What happened to you?"

"I let her out," he moaned as Rogers helped him to his feet.

Captain Burke favored him with a stern expression. "Who did you let out?"

"The woman! The monster from Titan! She's alive!"

"Wait a minute," Analiese said. "Nothing could survive being exposed to such an extreme environment."

Burke growled, taking a step towards Register. "I gave strict orders for the cryotubes to remain sealed. You've put the ship at risk, Mr. Register."

Register's eyes grew large. "I... Oh Jesus, she's coming!" He felt her mind reaching out to him as she drew near and she wasn't alone. The four researchers called out, seeking to enslave as they were enslaved, to enthrall as they were enthralled. The rest of the crew felt it too for they stopped talking and turned as one to the bridge's entrance to await the creature's arrival.

Their cancerous light preceded them up the stairs and then they were among the crew, dazzling them with their toxic magic. O'Halleran saw his brother, lost ten years before in a military action. Maitlin saw her girlfriend, Analiese her college sweetheart. Rogers saw a patchwork quilt of every woman he ever desired. For Captain Burke it was his son. They went unquestioningly to their loved ones with smiles on their faces.

Only Register saw with unclouded vision. He watched, paralyzed, as the monsters took them into their frigid embrace and latched onto their necks with their crimson teeth. He heard them as they began feeding, not only sucking blood but sucking emotion and memory, the very souls of their victims. He saw the parade of siphoned lives passing through his mind in a maddening collage of experience. He screamed for release from the barrage and was granted his pardon a moment later. Silence reigned on the ship in its aftermath. He turned to look about and saw the monsters' number swollen, reinforced by the *Hope's* crew. All trace of the people they once were was gone, erased by the change wrought in their flesh.

"Join us..." said the thralls.

"Love me..." said their master.

And he did love her, despite all he had seen. He closed his eyes, listening to her voice, and Katy was there when he opened them. There was nowhere for him to run, nowhere he could hide from their minds. It was the end.

"Will it hurt?" he asked her as tears began to flow down his cheeks.

Katy just smiled. She opened her arms and Register fell into her embrace.

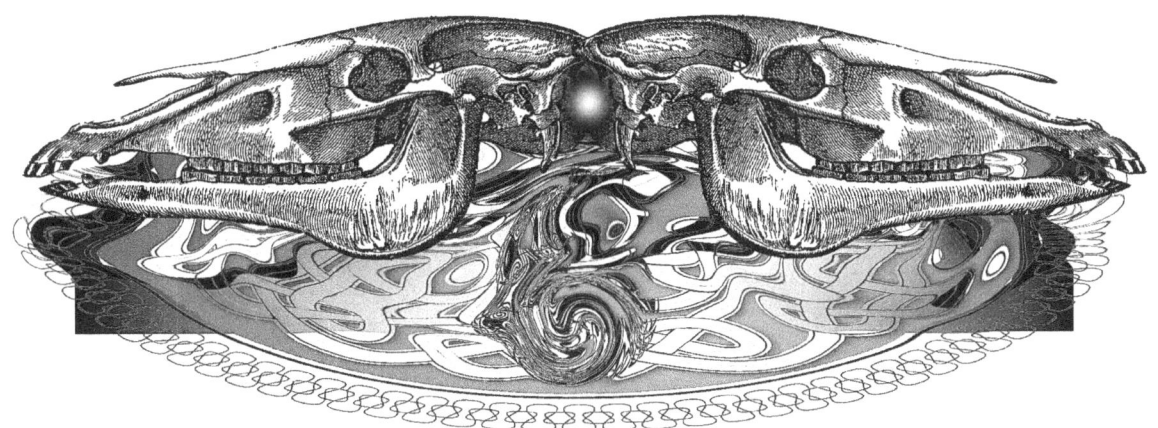

The Way of the Vines

Story by Marge Simon
Illustration by Paul Niemiec

"**Before a nuclear** holocaust wiped out most of civilization, the Vines were here. We think they were a species of ivy, mutated during the fallout.

Heart shaped, they writhed and twined around our feet. They spoke to us in their fashion, granted us their help in establishing a new social order. No such communication was received by our females. Clearly this was a sign that males were again to dominate society, with a few changes. On this most logical premise, and with the help of the Vines, we began to rebuild what was left.

The women worked and planted where the Vines allowed. When harvest came, we had enough to dry or store to see us through the winter. A rudimentary technology had survived, so education was left to us men, rather than our woman. Men knew more about such things. All that and more have become the way of the Vines.

When we men gathered for our singing time, we carried the little ones over our heads. To keep them safe but entertained, we passed them back and forth high above the ground. The Vines did not like the wail of babies or the cries of a small child. We did not want our children to come to harm. Our women were too weak or too busy to do what we could do, but they did not dare complain. They knew that was the way of the Vines.

It was good for us to sing our mating song. When we sang, the vines sent their leaves up and down with our voices. Those who weren't sure of their voices were quiet, and mouthed the words. After the singing, we gave our young to the care of our wives. For the next hour or so, pubescent girls were allowed to talk to us and touch us. Their fathers willing, such occasions often ended in a marriage pact. It was the way of the Vines.

I admit that sometimes when a wife angered me, I gave her to the Burial Vines. And that was a good thing. There were always more females than males, after the holocaust. Plenty to go around. I had several at a time, though not all men did so. Women are to respect and obey their husbands, as it should be. It was the way of the Vines.

Then Jenny was born, child of my own loins and sweet as sunshine. When she was three or four, it became obvious that she was hearing impaired. She didn't seem to understand what we said to her. Or rather, what I said to her. I doubted anyone would ever want her as a wife, they'd have too many problems communicating. I was sad, but I knew my wives would send good thoughts to her soul as they carried her little body to the Burial Vines. In fact, I was so overcome with grief, I didn't accompany them. It must be done, it was the way of the Vines."

* * *

Jenny turned off the ancient tape recorder and turned to her open-mouthed students. "So there you have it. That's my crazy father recounting our history. Questions?"

"Was that how it was, back in your day?"

"Indeed it was," Jenny smiled. "My father thought that women were fine with the situation. Do you believe that?"

The children, most of them girls, shook their heads. A boy raised his hand.

"Yes, John?"

"My mom says a girl talked to the vines. She changed how things were back then. They stopped telling our fathers what to do, right?"

Jenny gently disengaged her hand from one of the myriad vines that filled the classroom. It had already twined lovingly around her arm while she was speaking.

There was silence for a minute, and then a girl raised her hand.

"It was you, wasn't it? Your dad's wives didn't kill you, they knew what you were going to do when you got older right? You're the Vine Whisperer!"

Jenny smiled. "Yes, dears. The Vines soon realized, thanks to me, that women were the superior sex. We now have things rolling along very nicely. Men working in the fields and doing the hard labor. Women teaching, creating, bringing their energies to insure a new society, realizing our dreams—"

A buzzer sounded. The vines nodded and rose up to hustle everyone out of the classroom. and into their assigned cubicles. Including Jenny.

It was the way of The Vines.

Choice

Story by
Jude-Marie Green

Illustration by
Teresa Tunaley

Everyone on the settled world of Sasebo knew Gray's name. Few had ever seen her. Civilians gathered at the military base, held back by fences, but still hoping for a glimpse. Military personnel gathered too, in the administrative halls. She was supposed to be awarded a medal today, but the rumors said she'd never make it to the podium. The Administrator had it out for her. The Administrator had lost a brother because of her.

The rumors also said she wouldn't let herself be seen. She'd be surrounded by security guards. She might even, possibly, not show up. Go AWOL. Become fugitive.

The officers and ordinaries gathered in the hall fell silent when she showed up. She arrived alone, without a single adjutant.

"She's tiny!" The words, uttered by a male voice, shattered the silence. Someone hissed at him to shush, which he did, red-faced, but the silence was broken. Observations were whispered back and forth around her even as she clacked down the middle of the hall.

"Tiny indeed!"

"That's only because you're so tall."

"Shorter than my wolfhound. She commands a starship?"

"Size doesn't matter. But look at that hair!"

They did look. They wondered how such a tiny woman could walk under the burden of that fantastic head of hair. Gray braids surrounded her head like a lion's mane, a full and stiff natural style that focused attention on her face. By the time she reached the end of the hall, they finally noticed her face. The whispering in the hall became a tumult.

"How did all that happen to her?"

Though Gray was a great topic of gossip, no one could explain the cheek scars and forehead tattooing, broken nose and tattered earlobes. Somehow the tattered skin belonged in a face with those eyes, those lips. No one ever forgot Gray's face.

She wore her blue field uniform. It played up her difference from the officers surrounding her, the men in brilliant white. Belakane s'Burkol, known as Gray, walked set apart from everyone else in the hall, a clear target for the bullet she expected that never came.

She spotted the clerk waiting for her in the hall. Combat ribbons decorated his uniform. She recognized the battles. He may have served under her at some point. She nodded. Yes, a minor enlisted man with a minor injury that earned him a clerkship.

"Admiral Gray, please, we are in this room."

She smiled at the nickname, Gray, given to her by countless cadets she'd trained and crew she'd captained. She'd survived until iron-colored hair, a rare feat for people of her world. The name suited her. And she liked it.

The clerk held open a door hidden behind the podium. She swept into the conference room. The clerk shut the door on the crowd of white-clad officers. Vernil, the administrator, ignored her entrance. He shuffled paper. Paper! The sound whispered through the room.

His desk, an enormous c-ring of gleaming stone, some rare granite, not iron, surrounded him. Immensely expensive but not ugly despite its garish over-demonstration of power. Runnels of liquid water played under the desk's expansive surface, glowing opalene. An artist, a master craftsman, had carved this work.

Had Vernil commissioned such a thing? Had he found it and bargained with its owner? Had he stolen it—not himself personally of course, that would be beneath him—but had he issued unrefusable orders? Rumors followed this man like a bad smell. The fleet lived on such gossip and the tales generally leaned towards the truth. Pity for the desk's previous owner flashed through her.

Gray's seat, held for her by the clerk, was set away from the desk and centered from the walls. She understood the message: her place was powerless and small. The chair was polished wood, low seat, high back, and flared carved arms. No desk or side table for refreshments or documents. She would not need them.

"Auntie, would you like water?" The clerk dared to speak without permission.

Vernil glared.

"This is not a social visit."

Gray flicked a glance at the clerk.

"No, thank you, nephew."

Vernil cleared his throat.

"You've made a real mess for yourself, Gray," he said. "You'll be lucky to get out of this without serving prison time. Perhaps even execution. You do know that is the price for disregarding orders?"

"Vernil, my old friend. Who are you to criticize me? I take lives on your orders. My standing orders also allow me to save lives at my discretion."

"These orders were explicit. Quell the uprising using the harshest means possible. You failed in your duty. The colony not only remains unpunished, but it thrives under the new treaty conditions. A treaty you were not authorized to offer.

"You overreached, Admiral."

When she stood, Vernil flinched.

"I accomplished my ordered objective. The colony is subdued, the manufactory repaired, trade restored. Rebellion put down. With the added benefit of clearing that sector of coyotes."

"You violated operational policy and negotiated a treaty without authorization. Explain yourself!" Vernil realized what he'd said a moment too late. He held out his hand as if to capture those two words and unspeak them.

Gray smiled. She seated herself and folded her hands primly in her lap. "At your command, then, I invoke the right to explain. You must hear me."

The pink scars on the palms of her hands itched. She refused to look at them.

"My grandmother gave me the magic," she said. "She was too weak to do it alone. I helped."

* * *

We were hungry.

The horse lay on its back, squealing and flailing its legs, its enormous gray belly exposed. Four men sat on its neck. A woman lay across its head. Ancient women—not many, we'd buried most of our elders during that long season of plague and drought and famine—struck at the horse's limbs with rocks and tree branches. They laughed when they beat the horse, a laugh tinged with madness. Madness raged with the men who still owned sharp weapons, Bowie knives, bayonets rusted from neglect after being abandoned by careless soldiers, lengths of rebar appropriated from delayed construction projects. Their mouths spewed foam as they laughed and ripped the horse open.

I used a broom against the horse's tail. My hands stung as the new scabs broke loose. I'd given Grandmother my hands. She hadn't asked or reached out. I offered them.

I hadn't understood what I offered, but she needed help. She'd spent a week wandering the village, not talking to anyone. She picked up stones, branches, bits of cloth. I saw her sniff at a dog turd before returning it to the earth. Others thought she'd caught the madness of starvation. Not me. I knew she sought a way. So I offered my hands.

"Too young, too weak," she muttered, "but enough. Enough." She turned my hands over and over again and rubbed them as she sank into a daze, singing, a toneless whisper at first, gaining volume as she continued. She screamed, "Hai!" and rubbed my fingers cruelly hard. I should have cried. I didn't. I was far from the distress in my hands and began copying Grandmother's syllables, words I sang without understanding.

The third time she screamed, "Hai!" she cut. I don't know what she used. It looked like a blade of grass. Across both palms, from side to side, she cut. Along each hand, from wrist to fingertip, she sliced.

My stomach dropped. The exultation that seared through me forced me to stand. I screamed. Blood pooled in my cupped hands. After one last shout Grandmother tilted her head back and I poured my life stuff onto her face.

The war horse pranced into our village the next night.

Do you think of my world in golden tones? Even in the depths of that famine: yellow sun, amber grass, green trees. A vacation paradise, for a while. I've never returned. I think of my home and see only blood.

I was ten. The others beating the war horse tolerated my presence as much as they could not see me. I thought the tail end was a safe position. I was small enough to dodge the hooves and still fast enough despite the hunger that tortured me whenever I forced my muscles to work.

The horse sprayed urine and screamed. Blood spurted from its savaged belly. The hot stink excited me. It smelled of nourishment in the raw. I shook as I hit his tail again with the broom.

A crazed man, one of my brothers, grabbed the horse's testicles and pulled. A sweep of his hand and a barber's razor did its work, cleanly removing the horse's balls. A spout of blood squirted across my face. The horse screamed again, one last time, and a rear hoof caught me in the belly and knocked me aside.

My brother did not spare me a glance. He laughed again and threw the testicles into the fire. The smell of burning horsehair and burnt blood and flesh assaulted my nose and filled my mouth and I gagged. I could not vomit up what was not there but my muscles cramped and I lay on my back, holding my injured stomach, coughing vomitus. The horse's blood dripped between my lips. I sucked it in. The blood stung my lips and cheeks. I wiped my face with my hand and licked the blood clean from my palms.

I lay still, a few feet from the carcass as my village butchered the war horse. The smells played like a symphony against my skin and nostrils: the stink of shit, the copper smell of thick blood, the wet white squish and odor of intestines dragged from its body. Pieces of the horse were thrown on the fire: hooves with the repulsive scent of burning hair, hide that sizzled and seared, bone and meat that smelt raw and awful at first, like decomposing frogs, but then the aroma changed to the enticing scent of cooking meat.

We were all hungry. I was hungry. Still I could not bring myself to collect my share of the roasted horse.

My grandmother kicked me. Gently enough. She was not a cruel woman.

"Get up," she said. "You must have your fill before it is all gone. Or it will all be for nothing."

I tried to roll to my feet. The tattered and brightly-colored shirt twisted and rode too high, exposing my famine-swollen belly and my skeletal chest. The khaki skirt, too large for me by far, I'd tied with some rope, but that belting failed and the skirt slid down to my knees.

My grandmother kicked me again. "Cover yourself. Get your share. Don't worry about the horse. It will come back. Get some food," she repeated, "and I will tell you about this creature."

She smiled when I got to my feet. I pulled my clothes into some kind of order: the shirt down and tied with a knot, the skirt up and belted around my belly. The adults were strangely quiet while they feasted and no one spoke when I used my brother's ka-bar knife to cut an indeterminate hunk of meat from the pile of cooked horse parts spread on the ground. I looked at my grandmother and she nodded.

I sank my teeth into the meat and pulled off a chunk. Juice and spit dripped down my chin.

I chewed. My hands hurt from the magic she'd summoned and funneled through me. A gridwork of deep scratches oozed blood that mingled with the horsemeat's juice. The cuts stung. I cried and thought I was upset about the horse. My grandmother lost patience with me and slapped at me. Not hard but any slap from her was too surprising. My mouth fell open with shock, though I did not lose the bit of meat.

"Show me your hands," Grandmother said. She rubbed her thumbs across the opened slashes. "It's the bargain we made just last night. War will come but that was inevitable anyway." She shrugged. "For now, it gives us its flesh to eat.

"Don't mourn the horse, girl," my grandmother said. "It's the full moon. It's the war horse. The bones will come together before morning and it will go on with its life. It will feed us for a full year before we have to pay the price. So eat. Get fat. You'll need your strength."

I saw her fate in her faded eyes. She was letting go of life now that her magic had called the horse. I turned away from her because I didn't want to know that she wanted to die. I ate my fill of horse meat. When I had licked the last drop of juice from my hands I flung myself onto the ground again, onto my back.

The moon glared full and ominous above me, promising dire consequences. Some traveler had spoken of the silver rockets that flew to the moon, taking people there, and suddenly I could think of nothing I wanted more than to be on the moon, on the other side of that accusing brilliance.

I did not know the power of a wish made under a full moon in the backwash of ancient magic. From that moment, I was marked.

This happened in my tenth year, the year before the war, when the world was filled with signs and the river water exploded where it met the ocean.

* * *

Gray paused. The year of her grandmother's magic, which saved her people for a time but cast her tiny country's piece of the planet into madness for decades. Magic had an enormous cost. Strong was the woman who could wield it. Stronger yet the woman who could survive the aftermath.

Vernil sneered at her.

"Horses? Earth-born horses on your dirtball world? Spin me a story I'll believe."

Not that he'd believe anything. She was past caring on that count, however. Weary of the constant ignorance he wore as a cloak.

"Yes, horses. But you must understand, this was not a horse you'd buy at the market. This was a ghost. Magic. We fed on a horse because that was the strange and strong and nourishing to us. Perhaps your people would have devoured a pig."

He caught the insult she'd so casually lobbed and his lips dropped open in rage. He spluttered to form an argument but she had already turned away, tired of him. Her memory called her back to that evil place, The Road of Ghosts.

* * *

No one else in the village starved that year. We could not know that the same magic had called up the same bargain in village after village throughout our country. In the thirteenth month the horse did not appear. War overwhelmed us. Starvation seemed an easier death than the bullets and fire, kidnapping and rape.

My village burned. The child soldiers in their filthy uniforms shot at anything that moved and everything that didn't. My village, my people, the houses and the gardens and even the cloth-wrapped wire fence, all were stung with bullets. Those soulless children pressed the triggers of their automatic weapons to hear the song of the gunfire, the only songs that reached their hearts any longer.

I escaped the massacre and the burning. I found myself walking the Road of Ghosts. This road, infamous outside our country and feared as a conduit of terrorists inside, ran from one side of the continent to the other.

I trudged along the road alone among all the other ghosts. Blood splattered my left leg, not mine. Dried mud coated my face. I walked for days and nights, unending motion. When I could no longer walk I fell exhausted into the ditch at the roadside. I lay on the red dirt bottom without even the energy to swat at the flies that circled my head. The sun beat down on the shredded cotton of my dress, my legs, my head. I forgot all about starvation, about guns and fire, and I closed my eyes.

I woke to a man forcing my legs apart while another knelt on my arms. At first I thought I was blinded but then I saw the moon glowing behind the man's head. It gave him a halo and I saw his bones, his skull, instead of his dead eyes and stinking mouth. I knew what was happening. I'd seen coupling of animals in my village. My grandmother told me that I was too young but one day I'd want to couple with a man and that it would feel good. I'd like it, she said, and laughed when I asked my innocent questions of who and when and why.

I didn't like this. Pain filled me more thoroughly than the man's pizzle.

When the man's groans finished, he rolled aside and the other man put himself between my legs. I didn't make a sound, just watched the moon turn his face into a corpse's skull as well.

They stood and shared a cigarette.

"Should we keep her?"

"She's too small, she'd be a burden."

"Kill her then."

I scrambled to my feet. I was sore and injured but my terror propelled me. I ran. Too slow.

"Get her!"

The second man laughed and swatted at my head, knocking me into the mud. The first man dropped his cigarette butt onto my belly then slammed the stock-end of his gun into my head.

Much later.

The ground moved below me. And bounced. Dust rose from the feet of the man who held me slung over his shoulder. He was not one of my rapists. Short and bony, his face drum-tight. His skin smelled sweetly of honey. I hung with my eyes open and grew dizzy. I vomited onto his legs.

He didn't notice. He was walking, barely conscious, setting one foot in front of the other to keep moving on the road. His grasp on me was loose. I did not struggle. I'd rather he carried me. I would walk when he no longer could.

I dozed. At some point I heard the squeal of the war horse. I dreamt it, I know. Still, I opened my eyes. Three bodies lay arranged on the side of the road, naked to show the knife cuts and bullet wounds. Two men and a woman. The men's faces shined like bleached skulls under the sun. They were my attackers. I didn't know the woman and I didn't care. I smiled and closed my eyes again.

I don't know how many hours the man walked, the clockwork of his feet on the road lulling me to sleep and the jolt of his legs waking me over and over again. I only know that it was dusk when he collapsed.

He rolled onto his side and I fell off his shoulder. I rubbed his arm but he did not respond. His eyes were not closed, the lids open just enough to reveal the yellowed edges of his eyeballs. A machete wound traveled from his shoulder to his chest. It was shallow but had bled in a red sheet that spread down his torso.

I don't know if he lived. I don't think he was alive when I stood up and began walking.

The Road of Ghosts led nowhere and everywhere. I became one of the ghosts. Sometimes food appeared: a bowl of rice, a piece of fish, take a bite and pass what remained to the next person. I do not know where I walked or where I wanted to go, I merely moved to put the bad things behind me.

One morning … I was certain it was morning because the heat had not seared its way into my skin yet … I woke from my daze to find myself pushed into a line with a dozen other people. I fiddled with the scars on my hands, rubbing them, and sang one of Grandmother's songs, a summoning. I didn't understand what I was summoning. I forced my eyes to see, my mind to notice what was around me. Boys with rusted automatic propellant guns, wearing different tattered uniforms from the boys who'd destroyed my village, waved us to a stop.

A nervous boy, my height and shaking like a terrified dog, hit me with his gun. I swayed, humming under my breath.

I understood my magicking, then. I was summoning help. I'm not sure what I expected: the war horse, perhaps, come to protect me from the bullets. Grandmother gave me her art but not enough practice. In my exhausted condition, I could not control what might arrive.

In fact, no rescue arrived. No help.

Blood welled up from the split opened scabs on my palms. I rubbed the blood into the cuts on my face.

Blood overwhelmed my senses. It was all I could smell. I no longer smelled sweat, shit, the stink of unwashed people, or the mud of the dew-rinsed countryside. The blood was in my nostrils and my mouth, the coppery taste of meat. Blood soaked my skin and rushed through my ears like a constant lion's roar. My eyes filled with blood and all I saw was red.

And like that everything stopped.

The ghosts lined up next to me froze, slouched in defeat, motionless. I spared them a glance then concentrated on the soulless children in front of me.

They also were frozen but not dead as I'd hoped. The nervous one's eye twitched as I watched. A fly circling his head beat its wings in time to the thrum that roared in my ears.

I snatched the gun from the nervous one's hands.

Everything was red.

I stitched the boy soldiers' bodies with leaden fire, discharge from the gun. They crumpled, fell backwards, slumped sideways, in a gorgeous slow motion dance.

I smiled.

The road ghosts disappeared. I was alone with several dead boy soldiers. My vision cleared and the thrum in my ears subsided. I breathed in the full stench of the place again, shit and blood and dust, the rot of death and the stink of the yellow sun.

My foot was wet. The nervous boy hadn't died. He'd only fallen to his knees. He was trying to spit on me and the spray had landed on my foot.

I had his weapon, a rusted gun. It comforted my ragged palms.

I saw him clearly, the scraggly filthy bloodstained boy. Not much older than me. I could see into his eyes as he knelt.

"Look at me," I said. Soft as my grandmother's song. Soft female musical voice. He raised his head. His empty earth-colored eyes met mine.

"Goodbye."

I shot him.

* * *

"So you admit to murder."

Vernil's overacted shock vied badly against his smug face.

"I admit nothing," Gray said. "This is my story. You demanded I explain my actions. The boy's body brought your attention to me. The militia scooped me up, kept me in the same stinking hold as that boy's body...."

Her smile froze the air in the room. The clerk turned away from her and made a warding sign.

"I might have used my grandmother's magic to bring him back. Not all the way, of course, but enough so I could kill him again. And again. I might have played with his corpse until nothing was left but tatters of meat and bone.

"But I didn't do this. He was dead. Beneath my notice. The militia noticed my restraint. In their eyes, I advanced from possible problem to interesting problem. To solve me, they recruited me.

"They plucked me up with no sense of who I might have been and stuck me into a category, like hot plastic injected into a mold: military because I held a weapon, space because I'm small, combat because I'm fierce."

"All of this is in your psych record," Vernil said. "Your irrational belief in magic, your association with your country's marauding militias, your recruitment and all your training. This is not relevant to the charges against you."

"You speak of charges," she scoffed. "What charges? Name them." She stared at him, calm as stone.

He slapped his desk. "Murderer!"

"Oh please. A mere eight years ago I came to your notice. I became your personal knife. Is this also in the record? You assigned me to a series of, shall we say, delicate operations that required no sense of restraint along with an ability to do what I was told, no questions.

"And why should I question? I have lived my life without question."

* * *

My spaceship was like my home on Burkol. A ridiculous idea: a clean vessel like my filthy mud-struck home, yet there it was. I was comfortable surrounded by steel and plastic, familiar with all the halls and easeways and hidden spaces that made up the being of my ship.

I had my own personal space, a hidden cul de sac not far from my official quarters but impossible to reach accidentally. With the locator chip and telemeters I knew I was always within reach of my officers. I felt more hidden away and alone when I retreated to my indlu, my place. Often I heard my grandmother's voice there. More often, in fact, the closer we got to Indio Colony.

We, my crew and I, seldom needed use of arms to quell whatever insurgencies arose in the colonies. We'd made a name for ourselves: no one challenged Gray's crew. Strategies and tactics and honed teamwork. We'd done it all before. We were good. And we were bored. Everything was too easy.

Indio Colony seemed to be an average problem, an easy job. Destroy the satellite system, blind the colony's comm center, disable any ships in orbit or in parking, gas the colony's living spaces. Standard operation to quell a rebellion.

My crew was well-trained and deep into the first phase of the operation when I arrived on the command deck. The satellites were being picked up for physical rehabilitation. Not a difficult process.

But my second sweated when he reported.

"There are not enough satellites," he said. "A colony this size should have at least a dozen and in fact they have 22 registered, but we've only located eight of them and retrieved two so far."

A crackle of distorted sound exploded from the comm desk. Some of my crew startled from the noise. I noted their names for additional training.

The comm officer cleaned and amplified the signal and we all heard the words from the colony.

"We are in distress here and need assistance. SOS. Various systems have failed and we are open to space. Please send help! SOS."

"Record but do not respond," I said to the officer. "Find the signal origin. We'll start the gassing operation there."

"Aye, ma'am," my officer replied.

"Now, where are the rest of the satellites?"

"There's no additional signal."

I thought about it. If they'd known we were coming, they might have masked the signals, which we'd easily discover, or manually shut down the satellites.

"Go to visual," I said. No one groaned, though I might have when I was in their position. Visual inspection of the airspace around an entire colony—Indio Colony was built into a middling-size asteroid—took eye-wracking concentration and enormous amounts of time. Missing a visual clue was far too easy.

My first officer called up three ensigns and assigned them to screens. Each would visually scan the same area at the same time. The only way to be sure.

Bored, I turned from that problem and nodded towards my own screen.

"Give me a view of the ships in orbit," I said.

"None in orbit, ma'am," he responded.

I paused. That was unusual to the point of unbelievable. There were always ships in orbit. Someone must have warned Indio Colony we were coming. Damn.

"The parking deck, then," I said, striving for calm. The colony couldn't be abandoned, could it?

"Comms, that distress call. Was it a recording?"

"Not recorded, ma'am. Live signal."

I studied the view of the launch deck: empty of vehicles. The stand-by area, not down into the rock but sequestered to the side, showed a few varied craft, from personal skiffs to one lumbering cargo shuttle. Not as many as I'd expected.

Then I saw what I did not expect. I gasped and wiped at my suddenly-damp eyes. I looked again.

"Zoom in on that image," I said. "The ... the...." I could not say it.

"The horse, ma'am? Aye, ma'am." Comm's voice remained neutral.

On the other hand, I was surprised. And somewhere in the pit of my stomach, scared.

Between the ranks of the parked spacecraft a huge horse paced. Don't think that this was some phantasm of my mind. The view was recorded.

This creature stood 16 hands high at its metal withers, all exposed wires and lines and gears showing perhaps the tiniest flowers of rust, which to me looked like traceries of blood. The horse's nostrils flared eternally in a wide metal scoop. Its teeth shined of brushed steel, black metal lips pulled back to expose the horse's lolling tongue of plastic-robed wires.

Its shoulders gleamed with layer after layer of clockwork, pins, gears, and grooves somehow powering the thing's gold-plated hooves. The tail and mane flowed with waves of more knotted wires, vari-colored wires tipped with small plastic connectors.

Its flank bore the numeral 12, a lurid tattoo of baroque cast iron seamed into the metal.

As I watched, the thing galloped to the port hatch and reared up on its haunches, slamming its enormous fore-hooves against the sealed door.

The hatch opened.

Colony people in vacuum suits poured out, fell onto the horse, and ripped it apart. I saw hand torches and bolt cutters and wrenches used against the horse. I saw someone reach into its gaping stomach and remove a roll of reflective silvery Mylar, sealant against air leaks. Others pulled its head from its neck and legs and even the tail was cut off and tucked away.

When they were done, only the black numeral 12 remained. Discarded. Sprinkled with rust.

By now I was panting and even my best trained officers had paused in their work to stare.

The horse of my childhood, resurrected. The 12th month of its calling. The promise of the inevitable war to follow. Who among the colonists had used my world's ancient magic?

"You, Ensign," I said. "Access Indio Colony citizen base. Cross-reference with homeworld Burkol. With family name...." But I could not think of a name, not a single name, of someone from my homeworld. I'd never met a survivor.

"No results, Captain," the ensign responded. She was a sweet child, strong and smart and capable, a graduate of academies and tough training. Not someone who'd credit magic. Her mind was undoubtedly trying to impose a scientific rationale on the machined war horse's reality.

I knew better than that. I knew the magic. I knew the course of that magic and its inevitable horrific end. I never thought I'd experience it again. Now I'd be the bringer of war, forced by the magic.

Not that it mattered now.

They had made their bargain.

And I had my role.

I drew breath to issue orders. Hard orders. I tried to ignore the sting of magic that raced along the scars in my hands.

"Cap, coyotes on the horizon."

My attention snapped away from magic and destruction.

"Screen," I said.

"Can't see them all, we've pulled the satnet."

"How many?" I growled. Should have been easy enough for him to come up with a number. We had two points of reference, our ship and the colonized asteroid. Gravitational bending and field distortion would give a more reliable figure than just visuals from satnet.

"Five here, one hiding on the far side, and a big baby skimming close to the structures."

Under our ship's nose a lumbering cargo ship strafed the colony with physical bombs dropped from low orbit.

The young ensign, emboldened perhaps by my earlier orders to her, spoke.

"What are they after?"

Later I would rebuke her for speaking out of turn. Good question, though. I frowned.

"Nothing. They're never after anything."

I reviewed what I knew of Indio Colony. Successful enough, built on an asteroid. A port for trade, asteroid mining for precious metals, manufactory of some necessary goods, slow-building unique folk arts, determining their own future.

I nodded my sudden understanding. My mission of destruction was a lesson. They were to be taught obedience. Before me, an embargo. Had the coyotes managed that? A terrible thing, being cut off from the supply lines. Somehow they'd survived an embargo. No, not "somehow." Magic. The very magic of my homeworld. The magic of the war horse.

My grandmother whispered in my ear. I couldn't make out her words but I knew how I felt in my heart. I no longer wanted to be a pawn of the magic.

I made a decision.

"Comm, hail the coyotes," I said.

He acknowledged the order. I was barely conscious of the low drone of his voice until he spoke to me again.

"Cap, head coyote on voice. No visual."

Was he hiding or just poor? I decided to use this lack. I flicked battle signs to my crew, ordering a certain maneuver.

"Cease and desist," I said. "We are Navy Protectorate. Indio Colony is under our protection. It will be bad for you if you continue your attack."

"But you were sent here to give us cover!"

"Give me your name, captain. We should talk before you go too far."

"I am Blackbeard," he said. "Who the hell do you think you are?"

I accessed data records for his name. "Blackbeard" came up a few times with an interesting ancient entry. A pirate. Feared and despised. I rolled my eyes. He stole a name rather than make one for himself. I signaled my crew. They worked together like a linked unit. As one, dozens of high-energy weapons fired on the coyotes' fleet. My small ship had roared again.

"My name is Gray," I said. "I will accept your surrender now."

The expected moment of silence as the coyote

captain absorbed the information. Someone in his crew was telling him that we'd just disabled his ragtag fleet.

"Gray," he said. "An honor to be defeated by you. We yield."

"Do you require assistance?" Never leave an injured enemy behind. Kill or consume.

"Now that you mention it." His voice sparkled over the comm channel. One of the data entries mentioned his charm. He'd be a perfect ambassador.

The political officer chose that moment to protest. He stood up from his station, hands on his hips.

"Your duty is to destroy the colony, not make nice!" he shouted. "I'll report you!"

My crew stopped cold. The weight of their eyes was heavy. Their resolve could crack at any moment. My crew, yes, but they knew I'd broken from orders. From expectations.

They learned then that my sidearm was not decorative. I shot him.

* * *

"Yes, I used a projectile weapon in a spaceship. Still, he presented a perfect target. Only later did I learn this man was your brother, Vernil. I understand why you condemn my actions.

"I created a treaty. You won't understand this, but my soul couldn't withstand the debt of so many more deaths.

"You sent a war ship and meant for me to destroy that colony as a lesson to any others who might try for independence. Instead, I replenished the stores, recruited the coyotes as a home guard, and stood watch until the diplomats worked out a treaty."

Gray paced the width of the room, her eyes on the floor. Vernil did not interrupt her thoughts.

"Have you ever wondered about the cost of magic? A little piece of my grandmother's soul disappeared every time she cast a spell. Something evil consumed it and spit it back out, corrupt. When it came time for war, she had no soul left. No fight.

"I wore my grandmother's magic for the good of my family, my world. I've used it, spells, calling on the gods, during the course of my duties with you, Vernil. Your requests were fulfilled with magic!"

She shot an amused glance at him. He stared back, stony-eyed.

"And every time, I felt a bit of my soul eaten away, a bit of my self corrupted. Helping that colony cleansed me. Cured me, maybe.

"My grandmother was dead. She was beyond caring these many decades ago. My own soul is mine.

I pay the price I need to pay.

"I knew I could save that place. Those souls. Without magic. And so I did."

Vernil sneered at her again. "Magic! Souls! We are talking about contravening orders, purely black and white, nothing mystical here. You disobeyed. You will be publicly court-martialed and broken."

Gray sat again.

"Do what you must do," she said. "I did the right thing."

He slammed his broad palm hard on the polished table.

She didn't flinch.

"That was my brother," he said.

"Yes," Gray said. "I'm sorry I brought you pain."

"I know what they call you: The Old Gray Mare," he sneered. "It's time you were put to pasture."

He stomped out of the conference room.

Gray breathed deeply, staring at her hands. Even after all these years, the scars throbbed. She rose from the chair. Perhaps she should consider retirement. More ached than just her hands.

The clerk waited, eyes darting up at her and back down to the floor again.

"You'll retire with full honors, Admiral, despite what Vernil says," he whispered. He would not meet her eyes.

"How would you know anything of this?"

"My family," he said. "They live on Indio Colony." He glanced at her face. "Thank you, Auntie."

He opened the door for her. "They're waiting for you."

Vernil stood at attention next to the podium, an artificial smile pasted on his face. A distinguished elder politician leaned against the podium finishing her remarks to the assembled ocean of white uniforms.

"This decoration could not have been more deserved nor this honor bestowed on a better recipient. Please let me introduce Admiral Belakane s'Burkol, the Hero of Indio Colony."

Applause erupted, garnished with whistles and echoing cheers. Gray squared her shoulders and joined them at the podium.

dark matters

when the world was flat
we knew where we stood
on terra firma like a tower hill
the sun above to light our works and days

what a trauma then to yield the stage
to fissiparous atoms and fizzier particles
that cannot decide where they exist

our sun proved middle-aged and mediocre
our earth maybe one of hundreds
of billions of worlds that spin

next we discover that most of matter
we cannot even detect or measure
though it may hold
the scaffolding together

so are we in fact irrelevant
the product of bare chance
just insects feeding on dust and dreams
our brilliant lights but a cosmic
pinpoint

yet poor words
retain a faithful magic
even feel

— Anna Sykora

Book Reviews

Terence, Mephisto, and Viserca Eyes
Chris Kelso
Bizarro Pulp Press
$9.99, Trade Paperback
142 pages

In *Terence, Mephisto, and Viscera Eyes*, the reader is thrust into a bizarre world where nothing is quite right, and it almost seems as if it should be that way. This world, known as the Slave State, unfolds in nine short stories that are not for the faint of heart. The opening story, "The Family Man," is only a page and a half, yet the sheer brutality described therein sets a tone for the rest of the stories. The title story is told from the point of view of a mistreated dog who, after being castrated, is overcome with the desire to be a writer. "Baptizm of Fire," set in surreal version of Lagos, Nigeria, descends into a nightmare of both love and murder that pulls the reader deeper and deeper into the horrors of the Slave State. And when the reader finally reaches bottom, the incarnation of the bestial Slave State stares back with eyes dripping with viscera.

Few books have disturbed me. And of those few, none have disturbed as Chris Kelso has in this collection. From the bizarre atmosphere evoked from the first page, all the way to the final, horrific transformation in "Birth, Sex, Death, Stigmata," I could not stop the mental cringes. The dark imagery, the emotional punches to the groin, the utter emptiness of the loss of control... Dread lurked on every page, yet I had to have more, as if I were searching for hope, though all the while knowing I would never find it.

"Baptizm of Fire" was the blood-curdling and thought-provoking standout of an amazing collection of bizarre fiction deserving of five talismans. If the lasting, disturbing impression this collection has made on me is any sign, Chris Kelso will soon be a major presence in the genre. One that should be feared.

— Kurt MacPhearson

Space Traveler
Benjamin S. Grossberg
University of Tampa Press
$14.00, Trade Paperback
130 pages

I can't stop thinking of this as The Emperor's New Spacesuit.

There are sixty-six poems here reprinted from at least 34 academic journals and small press publications to wide acclaim. Benjamin Grossberg has published two earlier books which have won prizes and awards all over the place and he is Director of Creative Writing and an Associate Professor at the University of Hartford, as well as Associate Editor and book reviewer for *Antioch Review*.

The thing is, I just don't buy his Space Traveler. The second poem in the collection, "Wandering," tells us that the nameless Traveler built his ship out of odds and ends: "First appliances: fridge, stove,/ electric tooth brush and water pick." Then bigger stuff—siding, a chimney, water heater, bed springs. Much later, in "His Duende," he escapes a black hole by jettisoning "appliances, old/ furniture I'd hoped to refinish." Yeah, that's gonna work. Of course he's only speaking metaphorically, but I find it irritating, not poetic.

In poem after poem the Traveler visits planets all over the galaxy, lives for a while with an unnamed, faceless husband and then heads out again to travel space. Unfortunately, the space travel is as phony as those odd ends his ship was built from. Nowhere in these poems did I feel the Traveler was moving through the huge universe we're beginning to explore. Tellingly, the Traveler speaks of going "up" rather than "out" to the depths of space. Up is for us planet dwellers. Out is where the space travelers are "at."

So here comes the *Space Traveler* to great fanfare and hoopla—the crowd is going wild. Long live the Traveler! Sorry, all I see is that damn spacesuit.

— Neal Wilgus

Celebrate *Tales of the Talisman's* tenth anniversary this spring!

A woman copes with a troublesome pregnancy and the mortality of her mother. Melinda Moore shows us what the crows do.

Simon Bleaken reminds us that tennant rights have always been a tricky issue, especially when the landlord wants to use the tennants to replace his dead family.

Courtney Floyd introduces us to an Albuquerque private detective who has a penchant for riddles and supernatural mysteries.

What would happen if solar flares rendered all electrical systems useless. K.S. Hardy imagines the clockwork world that results.

Lee Clark Zumpe reminds us that the ghost of H.P. Lovecraft still haunts the world today.

These and other thrilling stories await in the spring issue of *Tales of the Talisman!*

We're taking a break soon, but you can still subsribe to *Tales of the Talisman* at www.talesofthetalisman.com today!

Pre-order volume X, issue 4 for $6.00 (That's 25% off the cover price)
Back issues available for $8.00 apiece

Visit hadrosaur.com for more great books and audio available from Hadrosaur Productions

Subscriptions also available by mail at:

Hadrosaur Productions, P.O. Box 2194, Mesilla Park, NM 88047-2194

About the Contributors

Lou Antonelli has had 83 short stories and three collections published in the past eleven years. SFWA-pro publications were in *Asimov's Science Fiction*, *Daily Science Fiction* (2x), *Buzzy Mag* and *Jim Baen's Universe*. He has eleven honorable mentions in *The Year's Best Science Fiction*. He was a finalist in 2013 for the Sidewise Award in Alternate History for "Great White Ship" (*Daily Science Fiction* - 2012).

Glynn Owen Barrass lives in the North East of England and has been writing since late 2006. He has written over a hundred short stories, most of which have been published in the UK, USA, France, and Japan. He also edits anthologies for Chaosium's Call of Cthulhu fiction line, also writing material for their flagship roleplaying game.

Ruth Berman's work has appeared in many sf/fantasy, general, and literary magazines and anthologies including *Hadrosaur Tales*). Her novel, *Bradamant's Quest*, was published by FTL Publications of Minnesota. She was one of the contributors to *Lady Poetesses from Hell* (Bag Person Press Collective, Minneapolis).

Simon Bleaken is a long-time fan of the Sci-fi, fantasy and horror genres. His fiction has appeared in several magazines and chapbooks, including: *Lovecraft's Disciples, Strange Sorcery, Night Land, Beneath the Moons of Zandor, Weird World of Zandor* as well as in previous issues of *Tales of the Talisman*. He has also appeared in the anthologies: *Eldritch Horrors: Dark Tales* and *Space Horrors: Full-Throttle Space Tales #4* and will also appear in the forthcoming anthology *Best Gay Romance 2015*. He is a supporter of Greenpeace, the World Wildlife Fund and the Stonewall charity, as well as a member of OBOD and British Mensa. He lives in Wiltshire, England.

Originally from the U.K., **William Corner Clarke** lived in Greece from 1989 until 1993. He came to the U.S.A. in 1994. His poems, drawings, and prose pieces have appeared in many magazines in the U.K., Greece, Canada, and the U.S.A. For the last 8 years William has been a regular contributor to *Waterways* poetry magazine produced by Ten Penny Players in NYC. A collection of his poems—*The Blue Sky Door*—was published in the U.K. some time ago. William has work in 4 anthologies, including the U.K. Science Fiction anthology *Dreamers on the Sea of Fate*. He is pleased to be able say that other poems of his have appeared in previous issues of *Tales of the Talisman*.

Gary W. Davis has published three gothic poems in *Tales of the Talisman* since the beginning of last year. He enjoys writing poetry about classic creatures such as vampires, mummies and werewolves. He recently penned a werewolf transformation poem, entitled "Brain-Sturm," that will be appearing in *Bloodbond* magazine this year. Mr. Davis also loves all things Halloween. In 2014, he wrote a short ghost story, "She Didn't Forget Halloween," and an essay, "Zen Philosophy for Halloween," which takes an Eastern holistic approach to some of the strange and diverse practices of Western Halloween culture.

Douglas Empringham has had fiction accepted by *Black Gate, Space and Time, The Lamp-Post, Leading Edge, The Armchair Aesthete, Rosebud* and other genre and literary magazines including both *Tales of the Talisman* and *Hadrosaur Tales*.

J Alan Erwine is a writer, editor, and RPG designer. He has sold more than 40 short stories to a variety of markets, and has also had three novels published, as well as several short story collections. He has been editing for more than a decade, and has edited several books, as well as being the continuous editor of the magazines *The Fifth Di…* and *The Martian Wave*. He is the co-creator of the *Ephemeris Science Fiction Role Playing Game*, and has written most of the supplements that have been created for the game.

When not overwhelmed by writing, editing, and game design, J spends time with his amazing wife, Rebecca, and their three wonderful daughters: Eryn, Juliah, and Alexis. To learn more about J, please feel free to visit his website: http://www.jalanerwine.com.

A frequent contributor to both *Tales of the Talisman* and *Hadrosaur Tales*, **Gary Every** is the author of the science fiction novella *The Saint and the Robot*, which is based upon a medieval legend concerning the youth of Thomas Aquinas. *Shadow of the OhshaD*, a collection of the best of his award winning newspaper columns about Arizona's Native Americans, history, and environment is also available at Amazon.com or his website www.garyevery.com

As a child, **Kathy Ferrell** refused to share her crayons, preferring to eat them all herself. Today she is an artist and writer working from her decidedly sinister 19th century home, nestled deep in the backwoods of Appalachia. When not creating, she can be found wrapped in a shawl, drinking tea and wondering what on earth could be making that incessant creaking on the stair. She also uses the internet, in spite of being warned.

Paintings: cuposwank.carbonmade.com
Words: cuposwank.wordpress.com

Neil T. Foster is a freelance artist who lives in Australia. He has penciled and inked various comic books, recently completing an online comic—*Beware the Beast*—for the official International *Planet of the Apes* Fan Club. He has done illustrations and painted covers for various SF fanzines, CD booklets and computer games. His work includes everything from illustration, cartoons, logos and comic strips to artwork for action figure packaging. His illustrations and painting have also appeared in *The Corpse* and *Black Petals* Magazines.

Laura Givens is a Denver Based author and artist. Her art has graced the covers of numerous publishers' books and magazines. She has provided illustrations for *Orson Scott Card's Intergalactic Medicine Show, Jim Baen's Universe, Talebones, Science Fiction Trails* and *Tales of the Talisman*. Her work may be viewed at www.lauragivens-artist.com. In 2010 she naively decided she could probably write stories as good as many she had illustrated. She has sold works ranging from zombie stories to space operas. She was co-editor and contributor to *Six-Guns Straight From Hell*, a weird western anthology, and is art director for *Tales of the Talisman* magazine.

Morland Gonsoulin is a traditionally trained artist and avid science fiction fan living in Colorado Springs, Colorado. He has done artwork for various publications before, including *Tales of the Talisman* Magazine.

Jude-Marie Green recently sold stories to *M-Brane Science Fiction, The Colored Lens, Insatiable*, and *Penumbra*. She is a Clarion West 2010 graduate and has the tattoo to prove it. She won the Speculative Literature Foundation's Older Writers Grant for 2013. She attends conventions when she is not huddled over her keyboard. Her wordpress site is at: judemarie.wordpress.com.

Tom Kelly received a degree in Graphic Design from Lycoming College and holds a master's degree in Sequential Art from the Savannah College of Art and Design. Tom has worked for several years producing graphic design and illustration for numerous design and production companies. As a freelance artist, Tom has produced illustrations and cartoons using a wide variety of classical and electronic techniques. Tom focuses on creating dynamic visuals by fusing together a wide variety of elements into one thought-provoking illustration. Tom's sequential work focuses on the power of bold black and white elements as well as the power of graphic design to relate a narrative.

When not writing poetry, **David Kopaska-Merkel** studies the rocks of Alabama. Kopaska-Merkel has written myriads of poems, stories, and essays since the 70s. He won the Rhysling award (Science Fiction Poetry Association) for best long poem in 2006 for a collaboration with Kendall Evans. He has written 23 books, of which the latest is *Luminous Worlds*, a collection of dark poetry from *Dark Regions* (Available at Amazon.com). Kopaska-Merkel has edited *Dreams & Nightmares* magazine since 1986.

Dreams and Nightmares website: http://dreamsandnightmaresmagazine.blogspot.com/.
@DavidKM on twitter.

Jag Lall works in both the comic book industry and book illustration field producing bold, atmospheric artwork. The former is his lifeblood and he is currently working on a project to raise awareness of different cultures.

Proud to be a frequent contributor to *Tales of the Talisman*, **Jim Lee** has been a freelance writer/editor since 1982. His recent publications include stories in *Mystic Signals, Dark Eclipse*, the Australian webzine *SQ Mag* and over in England, the erotic steampunk anthology *Valves & Vixens* (House of Erotica). His short novel, *Coyote Summer*, is to be published as an e-book by Crimson Frost Books and will be his first stand-alone book.

Mary Soon Lee was born and raised in London, but became a naturalized US citizen in 2003. Her poetry credits include the *Atlanta Review, Dreams*

& Nightmares, *The Magazine of Speculative Poetry*, and *Star*Line*. She has an antiquated website at: www.marysoonlee.com

Sandra Lindow lives on a hillside in Menomonie, Wisconsin, where she teaches, writes, edits and competes with wildlife for the pleasure and sustenance of her various gardens. Her book, *Dancing the Tao: Le Guin and Moral Development* (Cambridge Scholars, 2012) focuses on the development of moral maturity and was a finalist for the 2014 Mythopoeic Award for Scholarship in the Study of Myth and Fantasy. Recently she coordinated the SFPA 2014 Dwarf Star Poetry contest and edited the contest chapbook anthology. She was a finalist for the Rhysling Award twenty-one times. She has seven books of poetry. The most recent is the *Hedge Witch's Upgrade* (2012).

Kurt MacPhearson lives in Saginaw, Michigan with his wife and son. He modifies diesel engines into eco-friendly vegetable oil consumers while converting murky thoughts into something palatable. The former smells of french fries; verdict's still out on the latter. His stories and poems can be found in *Fantastical Visions V*, *Dreams and Nightmares*, *The Magazine of Speculative Poetry*, *Star*Line*, *Scifaikuest*, *Wild Violet*, and *Tales of the Talisman*.

Lyn McConchie continues to live and write on her small farm in New Zealand's North island. Her 32nd book (*Sherlock Holmes:Repeat Business*) appeared from Wildside in January, and her 271st story in the Australian anthology *Use Only As Drected* in June. Lyn shares her home with 7469 books and one Ocicat named Thunder. She continues to write, farm, and cuddle the cat, all occupations being equally important.

Erika McGinnis has been painting and drawing since she was very young. She earned her Bachelor of Fine Arts from Boise State University (go Broncos!) in 1998 with an emphasis in art history. Erika is a member of the International Association of Astronomical Artists (www.IAAA.org) and is an avid science fiction reader, from where a lot of her inspiration comes. Her art has shown at various scifi conventions around the country and has won "Best of Show" quite a few times. Erika instructs watercolor classes for the Idaho Academy of fine Arts and youth art through Young Rembrandts. She has done numerous illustrations for books, CD covers and magazines, such as *Farscape - Season Three*, *With Friends Like These*, and *Tales of the*

Talisman. Her **New Star Tarot Deck** and **Boxed Set** are available through Barnes and Noble and various online booksellers.

Erika owns a company called *Under the Cobalt Sky, Llc.*, which carries a line of products featuring her artwork for yoga wear with proceeds benefiting the Humane Society and jewelry that emphasizes the different ages of art history. These are available at museum shops and on-line on her website: www.erikamcginnis.com.

Erika lives in Boise, Idaho, with her husband, jazz saxophonist Sandon Mayhew and their dog, Thelonious.

Paul Niemiec plays guitar in a swing band—atomic pablo. Check it out at myspace.com. Paul's first job in high school was an art job doing safety filmstrips for hard-rock miners. After that, the office situation—smooth jazz radio, and chain-smoking co-workers—really put him off commercial art.

After a long hiatus, he got back into drawing. Paul was trying to figure out which way a camel's front legs bent, and he decided to go to the zoo to draw camels. Later, he met some of the Squid Works guys at a figure drawing class.

Carma Lynn Park has been reading and writing speculative fiction for (mumble, mumble) years. Much of her time is spent hunched over the keyboard for the inevitable day job as well as for creative work. She wants to thank her writing group for their advice and support.

Robert Redwine works in a sweatshop to support his writing habit. This is his second contribution to *Tales of the Talisman*. His work has also appeared in *Conceit* Magazine. He enjoys reading, watching too much TV, and tormenting player characters.

David B. Riley is the editor of numerous horror and weird western anthologies. He is also the author of four novels and more than 100 short stories. He writes horror, science fiction and steampunk and is an active member of the Horror Writer's Association. He also is publisher of *Steampunk Trails* Magazine. David lives in Colorado and works in the hotel business when he's not working on literary endeavors.

W.C. Roberts lives in a mobile home up on Bixby Hill, on land that was once the county dump. The only window looks out on a ragged scarecrow standing in a field of straw and dressed in WC's own discarded clothes. WC dreams of the desert, of finally getting his first television set, and of ravens. Above all, he writes, and has had poems published in *Tales of the Talisman*, *Strange Horizons*, *Apex*, *Space & Time Magazine*, *Mindflights*, *Shock Totem*, *Star*Line*, and others.

James Frederick William Rowe is a young and up and coming author and poet out of Brooklyn, New York, with works appearing in *Heroic Fantasy Quarterly*, *Big Pulp*, and *Andromeda Spaceways Inflight Magazine*. When not writing fantasy, science fiction, and horror fiction and poetry, he is pursuing a Ph.D. in philosophy and works in a variety of freelance positions. The poet's website can be found at: http://jamesfwrowe.wordpress.com

Marge Simon's works appear in publications such as *Strange Horizons*, *Niteblade*, *DailySF Magazine*, *Pedestal*, and *Dreams & Nightmares*. A former Rhysling winner, she also won the SFPA Dwarf Stars Award in 2012. She edits a column for the HWA Newsletter, "Blood & Spades: Poets of the Dark Side," and serves as Chair of the Board of Trustees. She won the *Strange Horizons* Readers Choice Award for poetry, 2010. Bram Stoker Award™ for Superior Work in Poetry with Charlie Jacob, *Vectors: A Week in the Death of a Planet*, Dark Regions Press, 2008, and another this year for *Vampires, Zombies & Wanton Souls*, Elektrik Milk Bath Press, 2012. Her poetry placed in the winner's circle of the Balticon Poetry Contest this year, for the fourth time in recent years. Member HWA, SFWA, SFPA. www.margesimon.com

Christina Sng is a poet, writer, and occasional toymaker. Her poetry has received several Honorable Mentions in the *Year's Best Fantasy and Horror* as well as two Rhysling nominations. She lives with her family and an enigmatic cat north of the Equator.

Anna Sykora has been an attorney in New York and teacher of English in Germany, where she resides with her patient husband and three enormous cats. To date she has placed 131 stories in the small press, and 335 (shortish) poems. Motto: eat your rejections like pretzels; they won't make you fat...

Frank Tavares is a writer and Professor of Communication at Southern Connecticut State University in New Haven. He's the author of the recently published collection of short stories, *The Man Who Built Boxes* (Bacon Press Books), and his work has appeared previously in a variety of literary journals including, *Tales of the Talisman*, *Louisiana Literature*, *Connecticut Review*, *Story Quarterly*, and others. Listeners to NPR would recognize his voice as the one heard for many years at the end of all network news programs, "Support-for-NPR-comes-from-NPR-member-stations-and-from…" Tavares is also one of the founding editors of *The Journal of Radio and Audio Media* published by the Broadcast Education Association.

Jeremy Terry is the author of the three novels: *Dreams of the Dead, Mirror, Mirror*, and *Wendigo*. His short fiction has appeared alongside the works of legendary authors and screenwriters Ramsey Campbell, Jack Ketchum, and Eric Red in collections from SSTpublications, Azure Keep Quarterly, Sabledrake Publishing, and Nightscape Press.

With over a million words in print **Patrick Thomas** keeps busy writing the fantasy humor series *Murphy's Lore* (*Tales From Bulfinche's Pub, Fools' Day, Through the Drinking Glass, Shadow of the Wolf, Redemption Road, Bartender of the Gods, Nightcaps* and *Empty Graves*) as well as the *After Hours* spin offs *Fairy With A Gun, Fairy Rides the Lightning, Dead To Rites, Rites of Passage*, and *Lore & Dysorder*. His Mystic Investigators paranormal mystery series has grown to include *Bullets & Brimstone* and *From The Shadows*— both with John L. French; and *Once More Upon A Time* and the upcoming *Partners In Crime*—both with Diane Raetz. He co-edited *New Blood* and *Hear Them Roar*. Patrick's syndicated humorous advice column Dear Cthulhu has been collected in *Have A Dark Day, Good Advice For Bad People*, and *Cthulhu Knows Best*. A number of his books are part of the set and props department at the CSI television show and have been spotted on the show. His urban fantasy *Fairy With A Gun* has been optioned by Laurence Fishburne's Cinema Gypsy Productions for film and TV. Drop by www.patthomas.net to learn more or find out about The Patrick Thomas Show mockumentary.

Originating from the UK but now residing in the Canary Islands, **Teresa Tunaley** finds more time to devote to her love of art and writing. For more than 30 years she has been doodling traditionally with pencils and dabbling with watercolors.

Along with published stories and poetry, she can be credited with award winning cover art and illustrations for author stories. Her work can be seen online and in print across the UK, US, Canada and Europe.

"I like to think that I am very versatile in my choice of subject matter—my new surroundings provide the inspiration for me to paint on a daily basis and the fact that others may enjoy my work gives me the confidence to continue."

D.J. Tyrer is the person behind *Atlantean Publishing* and has been widely published in anthologies and magazines in the UK, USA and elsewhere, most recently in *Steampunk Cthulhu* (Chaosium), *Tales of the Dark Arts* (Hazardous Press), *Cosmic Horror* (Dark Hall Press) and *Serial Killers Quattuor* (JWK Fiction), as well as in *Sorcery & Sanctity: A Homage to Arthur Machen* (Hieroglyphics Press), *All Hallow's Evil* and *Undead of Winter* (both Mystery & Horror LLC) and *Fossil Lake* (Daverana Enterprises/Sabledrake Enterprises), and in addition, has two novellas available on the Kindle, *The Yellow House* (Dynatox Ministries) and *Acting Strangely* (Jazzclaw Publishing).

D.J. Tyrer's website is at:
http://djtyrer.blogspot.co.uk
The Atlantean Publishing website is at:
http://atlanteanpublishing.blogspot.uk

Louise Webster graduated with a degree in Communication Arts. She wrote the evening news for a small cable TV company.

While staying home to raise her children, she wrote for many of the small presses. She has also written an article for a psychology book, a horticulture magazine, and her poem on Lake Ronkonkoma won a prize.

Louise has written for June Cotner's anthologies *Dog Blessings* and *House Blessings*, *A book of Toasts* and was published in *Nurturing Paws* and *Miracles and Extraordinary Blessings* edited by Lynn C. Johnson.

She is proud that her work has appeared over the years in *Tales of the Talisman* edited by David Lee Summers.

Neal Wilgus has been writing and publishing SF/F/H poetry and prose for more than fifty years in the US, UK, and Canada. Some of his poems have been nominated for the Rhysling Award given by the SF Poetry Association and he has shared third place several times for the Data Dump Award for best SF poem published in England. His short stories have won the Fiction Contest at *Oasis Journal* several times. He also writes satirical *Leak News Service* stories and reviews

book for *Small Press Review* and elsewhere. He publishes regularly in *Star*Line*, *Dreams and Nightmares*, *Tales of the Talisman*, *Monomyth*, *Poetry Cornwall* and elsewhere. His 1978 nonfiction book *The Illuminoids* is still in print.

Alessio Zanelli is an Italian poet who writes in English and whose work has appeared in about 150 journals from 13 countries. He has published four full collections to date, most recently *Over Misty Plains* (Indigo Dreams, UK, 2012).